Eugenia Kononenko

A RUSSIAN STORY

A NOVEL

The translation was made possible thanks to financial assistance
of Arseniy Yatseniuk "Open Ukraine" Foundation

Arseniy Yatsenyuk Foundation

Glagoslav Publications

A Russian Story

by Eugenia Kononenko

Translated by Patrick John Corness

First published in Ukrainian as "Російський сюжет"

© 2012, Eugenia Kononenko

Translation rights granted by Calvaria Publishing House,
www.calvaria.org

© 2013, Glagoslav Publications, United Kingdom

Glagoslav Publications Ltd
88-90 Hatton Garden
EC1N 8PN London
United Kingdom

www.glagoslav.com

ISBN: 978-1-78384-011-3

A catalogue record for this book is available
from the British Library.

CONTENTS

TRANSLATOR'S NOTE

In the preparation of my English translation of *A Russian Story* I have been fortunate in enjoying the close co-operation of the author throughout. Ideally, this is how all literary translations should be written, so as to ensure that the translator is enabled to realise the author's intentions creatively without overstepping them. I would also like to gratefully acknowledge the support of my Ukrainian colleagues Dr Bogdan Babych and Dr Svitlana Babych of the Centre for Translation Studies at the University of Leeds, who read the translation and made positive suggestions for improvements of detail. — *Patrick John Corness.*

Patrick John Corness is presently Visiting Research Fellow in the Centre for Translation Studies at the University of Leeds. Formerly a Principal Lecturer in Russian and German, with wide experience in translation and interpreting, he has specialised since 2000 in literary translation from Czech, Polish, Russian and Ukrainian. He holds the Silver Medal of the Faculty of Arts, Charles University in Prague, for achievements in the international dissemination of Czech scholarship and culture. His interest in Ukrainian grew out of several years of close involvement during the 1990s in EU-funded projects supporting collaboration between universities in Western Ukraine and Coventry University in England. He has contributed translations of modern Ukrainian short stories to *Ukrainian Literature, a Journal of Translations* (Toronto), *The Massachusetts Review* and *The Stinging Fly* (Dublin).

To the memory of my Mother

A friend of his mother's, Iryna Romanivna, lived in a pre-revolutionary building in Lviv Square, and when he was a child her home had a remarkable effect on him. Venetian windows that looked out on to the old part of town, high ceilings, paintings on the walls — everything was so different from what he had known at his parents' house at Vitryani Hory. Iryna Romanivna's accommodation was not self-contained; she had a room in a communal flat, and in addition to the main door there was another one which always remained closed, hidden behind a large bookcase. That door must have led to the neighbours' room in the communal flat. However, he used to think it led to some different world. When he first asked Iryna Romanivna what would happen if they opened it she whispered that if you did not do so carefully you might disturb some very powerful sorcerers!

Ever since he has been living in America, he has occasionally had dreams about that room, though he never consciously remembers it. He dreams of the gold stripes on the wallpaper, the tall windows and the roofs of the old houses beyond. Now he is pushing the bookcase aside and opening that mysterious door, to find himself in a neatly whitewashed, sparsely furnished room in a rural cottage; there is just a table with benches in the middle, reflected on the well-varnished floor as though in a mirror. He takes a step inside this white room and he feels an eerie draught. On the wall there is a sloping mirror — he must have a look in it. Then Iryna Romanivna calls him: "Zhenia, where are you going? Come back this instant!" He wakes with a feeling of deep sadness that he has missed seeing something extremely important.

1. A picnic on the prairie

On a clear October day a group of five people were unhurriedly munching away in the open air, on a hill amid the extensive plains of the American Midwest. They were sitting on folding chairs around a table, also a folding one, eating off plastic plates and drinking from paper cups. They had driven out a dozen miles or so from the university campus and settled down here on a hilltop in the middle of the prairie, leaving the car by the roadside.

The company consisted of two women, one of whom could be described as a woman a little over forty, the other as a woman well over forty, two men of similar age-groups and a teenager who was fifteen. The teenager, named Myroslav, was the common denominator of the group. The man and the woman a little over forty were his long-since-divorced parents. The woman and the man nearing fifty were the respective new spouses of his parents and it could be that this pragmatic lad enjoyed a better relationship with them than with his own parents.

"It's great that you and *maman* got divorced and that you both re-married," the son had told his father that morning, sitting in the car as his dad's wife Dounia Gourman drove them to the shopping centre. "How dull it would have been to share grandad and grandma's flat in Pushkin Street!"

The flat of his deceased grandfather Professor Nebuvaiko on Pushkin Street in Kyiv is quite large, not only by Soviet standards but even by post-Soviet standards. Now his grandfather has died,

Myroslav and his grandmother live in those four large rooms, just the two of them. Periodically, he goes to Camargue to visit his mother and her Thierry, who has a successful restaurant business in the south of France, or he comes here, to visit his dad and Dounia Gourman, a professor of Russian at the local university. The boy is now going to spend a whole year in the United States. He has already started attending a local school, and he is living with his father and Dounia. His mother has just come to visit them with her Thierry. Of course, they will not stay long. American homes have four bedrooms upstairs, but they were never intended to be separate living quarters. Actually, the very fact that the group consists of former spouses and new spouses means that even in terms of the cultivated correctness of American society they are not supposed to spend an extended period of time under the same roof.

Actually, what is political or any other sort of correctness? It means being able to keep yourself from boiling over when you are all seething inside. It cannot be said that in this company, which has just ceased its munching and is languidly watching swallows swooping over the prairie, the drive into the country had aroused a dormant whirlwind of passions. But old sparks are nevertheless sometimes rekindled, which is slightly disturbing. Only Myroslav remains indifferent. Perhaps this is because he is the only one amongst them who speaks all their four languages; the others know three and a half at the most, like his mother, who is considerably less proficient in English than in French. The rest of them know even fewer languages.

To begin with, Dounia tried to get them to agree on a common language at the picnic, because her husband, Eugene Samarsky, keeps exchanging Ukrainian phrases with his former wife Lada Nebuvaiko-Giono that Dounia does not understand, and this always puts her in a slightly awkward position. It is this lack of understanding as such that Dounia is concerned about, rather than the fact that her husband and his ex-wife still retain a residual common language. Not only in terms of Ukrainian, but in a somewhat broader sense.

Lada addresses Dounia as *Klava*, or even *Klavochka*. And Klavdia Nebuvaiko, who was always called Lada in Ukraine, answers to Dounia's *Klava*. When her son Myroslav heard this, he burst out laughing: "Klava! Klava!" — pointing a finger at his mother. As he explained to his *maman*, if you said "you Klava" to a girl in Kyiv it meant you were telling her "you're stupid." For a long time now Lada has been called Claudine by her Thierry, because to him *Lada* means a car, not a woman. And she had a good laugh with her son; then she recalled that when she was a schoolgirl *Dounia* meant something similar in young people's slang.

"My mother kept putting on the *Dounia-the-Spinner* record until she wore the record-player out," said Eugene.

"We remember your mother, and that record player too," sighed Lada with a broad, nostalgic smile. "Incidentally, there you have someone who would support your wife as an enthusiastic Russophile."

Lada was beaming with a nostalgic smile now. She used to tell his mother all sorts of unpleasant things, saying that everyone was fed up of her Russian classics, and mother did not suffer this in silence, as a matter of fact. So Lada, in order to avoid these injurious altercations, limited her contact with his parents to a minimum.

"She and Dounia, as it turned out, had entirely different views of Russian literature," sighed Eugene. "They clashed over this. So we were not too upset when Mom did not get the three-year visa which she was very keen to obtain, despite everything, after Dad died."

"Yes, it would definitely have been possible if you could have had a child," said Lada.

That is rather sad. Lada and Thierry were in fact planning a child. After living together for several years, they decided to cement their relationship and they were expecting a daughter.

But they had a car accident on the highway near Marseilles. That was five years ago. To give them support, Eugene and Dounia flew to Camargue for a few days. They sat by their hospital beds while they were on a drip. And on the plane on the way back they discussed the disaster that had befallen their French 'relatives'. As for Eugene and Dounia, perhaps it had been sensible of them not to plan a child. After all, there is the unplanned Myroslav, who needs so much looking after!

Dounia is surprised that, for some reason, the lad's sonorous name, which sounds good in any language, is not adopted in Russia. No hero of Russian classical literature, which Dounia is familiar with in all its boundless extent, bears this name. Myroslav himself is unconcerned about that. Russia is not involved in his plans for the future. And even if it had been, well, "Russia has so many non-Russians, like us!"– as his paternal grandmother enthusiastically recited from a poem by some minor Soviet poet. But the French Mi-o-slav, and the American My-ros, sound cool. He is grateful to his grandfather, the late Vasyl Tarasovych, professor Nebuvaiko, for giving him such a fine sounding name. And he also thanks his lucky stars that he has both a stepmother and a stepfather. Thanks to them, his life is far more interesting than that of those who live for years without a break from boring parents in the same tiresome dwelling, known sentimentally as their 'parental home'.

So Dounia, with the academic's inherent propensity for orderliness, hoped to establish a common language for the picnic, but it did not work out. The proposed options were English or Russian. Thierry does not know Russian and he does not want to speak English. But Thierry cannot be excluded from consideration, since in most cases it is he who pays for the dinners in the restaurants on the university campus. Lada does not want to speak Russian, even though she answers to *Klava*. What is more, Lada asked why the Russophile Dounia does not speak French, since the heroes of the Russian classics actually spoke it better than they did Russian. Dounia replied: *"Bien sûr,*

I speak French! It is not perfect, but it is acceptable." Eugene does not speak French though.

"Didn't you ever learn it?" Lada asked her ex-husband again.

"There was no incentive. Except for getting to know your new husband better."

Eugene, as an erstwhile adherent of Nietzsche, learned German after English, and he did quite well at it. But all the French he knew was what he had picked up from Lada while they were together.

So the table continues to be dominated by a lack of linguistic agreement; however that does not lead to overt conflicts — only weak flashes of distant lights. Like those that wander in the darkness of the prairie of an autumn evening, eventually dying out. But something inextinguishable still remains, no matter how proud the newly-weds are of their ability to form wonderful relationships with their ex-spouses.

Thierry put his hand on Lada's shoulder, but Eugene did not put his hand on Dounia's shoulder, and in Lada's eyes there is a scarcely perceptible flicker of triumph, which, it is fair to say, never disappears from the eyes of ex-wives when their ex-husbands see them in the company of their new ones. And in any case it was understood that she and Thierry were closer than he and Dounia were. But Eugene and Dounia had also developed a reasonably balanced relationship, never arguing, but never clarifying matters either.

"How beautiful!" exclaimed Dounia, looking at the road meandering amid the plains, and the swallows overhead. "I have been following this road for years, but I never tire of it."

Since the beginning of their relationship Dounia and Eugene have often come here to this hill, where even in the dreadful summer heat a breeze blows among the bushes. Eugene has been driving for a long time now, but the itinerary has never varied. Dounia said this place reminded her of the Russian steppe, which she had read so much about but which she had never actually seen, because the only places she had visited in Russia were Moscow and St. Petersburg. She had begun, apparently quite spontaneously, singing *Steppes and steppes all around.** When Eugene, feigning a similar spontaneity, took up the refrain *Among the steppes that are so wide,* ** although the Ukrainian *recitative* is much more intricate than the primitive Russian folk tune, Dounia fell silent, and she no longer sings *Steppes and steppes all around*, on the hilltop amid the prairie. Nevertheless, they continue to come here and bring guests with them.

Dounia would immediately mount her hobby-horse. Whoever their guests were, she would always start banging on about her monograph on 'Russian Sexuality', which she has been writing all the years she has been living with Eugene, considering it the main purpose of her life. In Moscow, everyone is aware of this still unfinished book, because Mrs Dounia Gourman-Samarsky of Midwest University has given papers at conferences in Russia, presenting the respective chapters of her study. Russian colleagues have written to tell her that the Patriarch of Moscow intends to pronounce that her monograph is anathema, but in all sincerity Dounia does not understand why. What is the reason for this curse? Is it really because she gave several papers at respected universities, convincingly arguing that only Russian nineteenth century literature can speak about everything without actually saying anything? On the basis of scant details found in Russian classical authors, merely suggesting the depth of certain chasms, Dounia made unexpected findings. With the scientific directness of an obstetrician-gynaecologist, she examines how the fall of Anna Karenina occurred and how the landowner Totsky corrupted young Nastasia Filippovna. Right now Dounia Gourman was working on what Mark Volokhov was doing in the gazebo with the young girl Vera in Goncharov's novel *The Precipice*.

---

* A Russian folk song

** A line from *Testament*, a cult Ukrainian song set to words by Taras Shevchenko

"And the way the Muscovite treated Kateryna,* that is of no interest to your wife?" asked Lada.

"We are not at Harvard," replied Eugene.

"What has Harvard to do with it?" said Lada, confused.

"Only at Harvard could you obtain funding to pursue research on Kateryna," explained Eugene.

At the beginning of his relationship with Dounia he heard the phrase *we are not at Harvard* almost three times a day. If he had really wanted to develop a specifically Ukrainian branch of Slavonic Studies, he would have had to establish personal contacts at Harvard! But here too, in this university in the middle of the prairie, where spirits of the past roam during autumn nights, glimmering like the eyes of mystical coyotes, there are quite good opportunities available to him, said Dounia, combing her wild red hair inherited either from her Irish mother or from her Jewish father, who came from a family of immigrants from Belarus.

Dounia does not speak Ukrainian, so again things turned out as she had feared, and this is actually the reason why she had tried to establish a common language at the picnic. Once again she did not understand quite correctly what Eugene and Lada were talking about and at an inappropriate moment she confirmed that she had indeed given a presentation at Harvard on Katerina Ivanovna's distressing intimate relationship with old Marmeladov, which she had discovered after reading that great novel by the great Russian writer for the nth time.

"Can you imagine it, Klava, they approved my approach!" Dounia's green eyes lit up as she, a provincial university professor — one from the Midwest at that — began to speak about her success at Harvard.

---

* Kateryna is the eponymous heroine of a poem by the Ukrainian national poet Taras Shevchenko, a village girl seduced, made pregnant and abandoned by a soldier of the Imperial Russian army, nicknamed *the Muscovite*. The poem *Kateryna* is a central theme of classical Ukrainian literature, interpreted as symbolising relations between Imperial Russia and colonial Ukraine.

During the intellectual conversation between Lada, Dounia and Eugene, Thierry became discourteously bored.

"Mme Gourman," he said, stressing the final syllable, "isn't it time we drove back for dinner?"

"Oh, it's only just five o'clock," replied Dounia in French. "Since when does a Frenchman dine at five?"

So Thierry stood up, dragged Myroslav away from the table and started a mock fight with him. After several blows the young man pushed his stepfather over and sat on him triumphantly, and Thierry immediately pretended to be dead. For some reason Eugene recalled that when he had fooled about like this with his late father during family picnics at Pushcha-Vodytsia near Kyiv, his mother had always yelled at them, saying they had gone crazy, because they had over-eaten and now they were going to make themselves sick. But Lada disregards the antics of Thierry and Myroslav. The lad's own father remarked that he and his son had long since lost that physical contact whereby a boy and a grown man enjoy jostling and sparring together. To be more precise, he and Myroslav had never had such contact.

However, although he does not spar with Myroslav like Thierry does, he communicates with his son in their native language, fulfilling his parental obligations even across the ocean — all the more so since, according to Myroslav, grandma Nina had become completely de-Ukrainianised; she had switched to Russian, saying that the late Nebuvaiko had foisted his Ukrainian on her. When Eugene lived at their house on Pushkin Street, his mother-in-law did not seem to have had anything 'foisted' on her; on the contrary, in family company it was she who gradually imposed constraints on her highly-placed husband. Eugene had no influence on the way his son communicated with his grandmother Nina. So at least he taught Myroslav not to switch to Russian with his stepmother, saying that she had an almost perfect command of Russian anyway, whereas his son did not yet have perfect English. So Myroslav, like Eugene, communicates with Dounia only in English.

But in the end Lada started speaking Russian with his stepmother anyway. She makes a show of being enthralled by the depth of her research; however, she actually makes fun of the enthusiastic Russianist, asking ridiculous questions that Dounia takes seriously.

"Now Dounia, how do you rate Ilya Oblomov's sex life?"

"I can rate it such as it was! I have written an article on that too," said Dounia, and her eyes lit up. "

And was that also at Harvard?"

"No, that was at Princeton, also a very prestigious university!"

"So you dig very deep, I see!"

"Yes. A great deal depends on sexuality. Almost everything! The Old Russians knew this long before Freud. But sexuality does not mean pornography, because then it would have no depth; it would be purely banal! The Russian classical writers understood this just as well as the French. Even better, actually."

"Dounia, what could you say about the relationship between Khoma Brut and the damsel?" *

"Oh, those are your Ukrainian lands! Nothing is quite as it should be over there! I'll just need some help from Eugene on this."

"So funding is available for Gogol, and not only at Harvard?" Lada put on a clever show of being keenly interested.

"So you are not working yet?" He interrupts Lada, fed up of her mockery of the artless Dounia. Somehow everyone — Lada, Thierry and Myroslav — finds it necessary to make fun of his wife.

"Better call me *Traven***," the young man told his stepmother when she shortened *Myros* to *My* and Dounia again failed to grasp what the cross-linguistic puns were about. She knew Gogol's play *The Inspector General* by heart, though.

---

* Heroes of the short story *Viy* by the classic Russian writer Nikolai Gogol, who was born in Ukraine. The action of this mystic tale takes place in Ukraine. Many other works by Gogol are based on Ukrainian themes.

** The name of the month of May in Ukrainian

But Lada doesn't work! She doesn't work, she stays at home! She is a little housewife in a big house, that's all! She had always dreamed of marrying a Frenchman, so she didn't want Myroslav, but she had no wish to be concerned with merely choosing curtains to match the wallpaper! She wanted to teach at the university! She wanted to master the Provençal language, which no one in Provence knows. All her classmates at the Faculty of French Philology who married Frenchmen had long since divorced. They had dragged their former spouses off from Ukraine to France. That was usually the case if they had learned to speak French. But look what happened to me! Yes, that's right! All the feminism of my youth went to pot, just like your love for Ukraine!"

"Like our love."

2. The best years of his life…

To concede that those few years at the turn of the eighties to the nineties were the best years of his life would mean accepting that nothing good would ever happen in his life from then on. He didn't want that.

So when was it that he had ceased to be sincere in his life? When he lost Lada? Or when he lost Ukraine — but did he? In today's globalised world you don't lose your homeland; it is subsumed in that universal globality. Occasionally, he would meet old acquaintances at international congresses. Some of them would come from Ukraine to give papers; some had long since been affiliated to foreign institutions.

Meanwhile, the years flew crazily by. They say that to emigrate is to be re-born. How old was he as an American? Not quite as old as Myroslav was now. And what did he have to look forward to? The cruise to the Galapagos Islands he and Dounia were planning for their Christmas holidays? The conference in the Azores where he had been offered the job of interpreter, a short time before that? Long gone are the days when the anticipation of future journeys aroused in him incredibly powerful sensations — you might almost say a cosmic shudder. The Ukrainian acquaintances he met around the world (he is bound to meet somebody in the Azores too) still find their long journeys mind-blowing. These journeys somehow prolong life, which proceeds on its way regardless of its quality. *You see, life will pass by just as the Azores passed by*, once wrote a

Soviet Russian poet he found unforgettable, although generally speaking that poet is half-forgotten; he was a favourite of his mother's — and probably still is.

The Soviet period in Russian literature was not Dounia's cup of tea. Dounia loved Russian nineteenth-century prose. But reciting Russian poetry at the top of her voice — so loudly that the window-panes rattled — that's what was in his mother's repertoire. He hadn't seen his mother for over five years. She had been a Russian literature teacher in a Kyiv school. She is retired now, and he sends her money by bank transfer. For over twenty years he has no longer listened to her views; he makes his own decisions about his life-style. The verse written by Russian poets, which she used to declaim with such enthusiasm as a commentary on everything that went on in the world or in their family, still resounds in his head — appropriately or inappropriately, as the case may be — rising to the surface of the mire which is the past.

I have instilled Rus[*] *into you — as if with a pump!* — mother would say loudly, quoting the ambiguous Marina Tsvetaeva, poking her finger at her son; there was some truth in that, actually.

Eugene was distanced from the Russia that had been *pumped into him* by his mother — indeed not just by her but by the entire Soviet way of life — thanks to Ukraine, entering his life like an eccentric lover, a woman you perhaps wouldn't marry, but would keep getting together with and breaking up with again until you died. One of you or the other. Well, it turned out that during his student years, traditionally considered to be the best of your life, he had had neither good friends nor a proper girlfriend. He began to experience all the powerful emotions of youth a little later, soon after the Soviet Union had begun to collapse and fall

---

[*] *Rus* is the historical name of the 9th-13th century Kyivan state, the cultural and political precursor of both modern Russia and Ukraine. For present-day Ukrainians, *Rus* is a poetic name for Ukraine.

apart. During his final year at university he happened to attend a party at the house of some friends of his, and suddenly he found himself in a world of true fulfilment. There were young men there who you could talk to all night, yet in the morning you would leave with the feeling that you still had more to talk about. There were attractive girls who were not dying to get married, unlike the girls in his year who would do so virtually at the first opportunity that came along. You could talk with them all night too, sometimes even forgetting how beautiful they were, although you could actually combine the one with the other. He stayed the night with a girl after the very first party, and this was the beginning of his national initiation. After that night, Ukrainian became the language of love for him. It was not Lada. The girl thanked him for the joy they had shared, saying she would always have pleasant memories of that night. They still continued to see one another. There was no second time; things do not always work out, do they? But they would exchange the occasional sultry glance or knowing smile. If anything like that had taken place with one of the girls in his year, the hysterics would have started the very next day after she missed her period, and then the parents would have crucified her if she didn't marry him as a matter of course.

Similar circles of sensible lads and trendy girls, trendy lads and sensible girls, formed and broke up again in the multi-million city of Kyiv, not only at the time of the collapse of the Soviet Union, and not only involving the Ukrainian language and Ukrainian ideas. But this was where he ended up, and they took him in. Ukrainian became a language of communication for him, practically for the first time ever, rather than the language of the classroom, of theatrical performances or of poetry, and that was brilliant. Perhaps this was in tune with the spirit of the times, as it was then that people started talking out loud about how under the Soviet Union Ukraine was wilting, weakening, deteriorating and becoming less and less relevant to the Ukrainians themselves. By no means was it 'flourishing and radiant' as well-paid Soviet

Ukrainian poets ingratiatingly chanted. These very same poets were already beginning to compose sentimental verse on the theme of change in society. Personally, he had no particular agenda in adopting new ideas; in the Ukrainian world he truly began to feel a kind of inner harmony and a will to live which he had never experienced before.

He had started writing poetry a long time ago, though he didn't consider himself a poet. The first verses he ever wrote were in Russian. Ukrainian rhyming verse was easier to compose, more melodious, and made more sense. Sometimes he can still spontaneously recall some of the lines he jotted down on the back of a notepad containing his addresses and phone numbers. He could sing any song without getting out of tune, although he wasn't endowed with a powerful voice. But singing in unison, when his friends' voices powerfully augmented his own — that was an incredible feeling. To this day he can hear in his head the sound of those songs from over twenty years ago.

His new friends not only spoke Ukrainian quite naturally, but they spoke with a cheerful irony on the topic of their own Ukrainianness. Strictly speaking, none of them was a native speaker of Ukrainian; all of them had at the appropriate stage in their lives begun their mumblings in Russian. It was a different matter with Ukrainian, which had become the language of their re-birth, a more fascinating language, more existential, the secret language of a select community. True, there were very few such people in the Ukrainian capital, even during the short-lived wave of patriotic fervour of those years. But their members were not outcasts or pariahs. On the contrary, they were a kind of nobility, though their biological origins were of no concern to them. They were at ease when speaking about their Russian or Jewish grandfathers and grandmothers and about their parents, bourgeois Kyivan conformists or Soviet careerists. He had first noticed Lada when she openly spoke about her father, head of the department of scientific communism, previously responsible for Soviet ideology at a fairly high level. We have the parents

God gave us, and they are the only ones we will have. So we have to form our own way of life.

Now he fully understands that his friends from those years also had their own no-go areas which they did not want to speak about; indeed they were unable to do so, even with their closest friends. But in those same years they revealed to him aspects of life which had been inaccessible to him in Soviet days. They did not speak only about national issues; that would have been boring. But they spoke about everything in Ukrainian, and at the time he felt that in Russian he would have been unable to discover the new meanings which were coming to light.

He began to pay attention every time he heard Ukrainian being spoken in the Russian-speaking hubbub of Kyiv's noisy streets, trolleybuses and coffee houses. He always listened in, to discover what kind of person was speaking. First there was a comical mixture of Ukrainian and Russian; the intonation is Ukrainian, but the vocabulary... In their social circles they indiscriminately parrot this hybrid speech coming from the mouths of the uneducated and the semi-literate. But these country girls, on the other hand, are speaking Ukrainian surprisingly well. This means they are from a locality where the Ukrainian-Russian hybrid has not yet become established. For them Ukrainian is truly their native tongue. But they are unaware how good their Ukrainian is; soon they will learn city speech, possibly even losing their rural accent. And here is a Galician with his characteristic vocabulary and intonation patterns. He too is speaking his native tongue. And this person he is talking with — generally a Russian speaker, as you can immediately tell — attempts to demonstrate that he is able to switch to Ukrainian quite readily, if necessary. But he keeps hesitating and making funny mistakes. And here is someone else — a kind of a Soviet establishment figure — who begins speaking Ukrainian in a loud, booming voice, with execrable accuracy, though certain elusive characteristics of his speech tell you this is the moribund language of Soviet Ukraine. Professor Nebuvaiko used to talk like this, by the way. And when Ukrainian is spoken without rural or Galician intonation patterns, with no clumsy Kyivan expressions or inane Soviet sentimentality, this is an indication that somewhere close by one of his own people is talking.

Later on, his associations with Ukrainian circles became less romantic; they were more pragmatic and they were firmer. His Ukrainian friends began to propose venues where he could give a talk or they found him an opportunity to publish an article, and he was successful in this. He learned to speak at round-table discussions and on the radio. And he also acquired skills in communicating with Russian chauvinists of varying levels of bigotry.

"You are absolutely right," he replied to a moronic Russophile on the first floor of the Art Shop on the Khreshchatik, who was objecting to the excessive Ukrainianness unique to Kyiv. "They don't let people read Dostoevsky! They play their patriotic Ukrainian *Red Viburnum** just when you are reading about Rogozhin's gift of ear-rings to Nastasia Filippovna in *The Idiot* — do you often re-read that? See what I mean? No-one re-reads Dostoevsky's *The Idiot*, but the damn nationalists know Nechuy-Levytsky's *Kaidash Family*** off by heart!"

The Russophile, who intended to have a conversation on the topic of the artificiality of Ukrainianness, which had no future, felt he had been fooled, since the Ukrainian nationalist turned out to be untypical. So the principled Russophile, denied the pleasure of conversing with an ideological opponent, gave up browsing his favourite bookshelves and fled.

"How did you manage that?" exclaimed Lada enthusiastically.

"Well, how can I put it? He himself can't distinguish between

---

* *Red Viburnum* is the title of a Ukrainian patriotic song frequently heard during street demonstrations in the era of Soviet *perestroika* and during the first years of Ukrainian independence.

** *The Kaidash Family* is a novella by Ivan Nechuy-Levytsky, whose works *Mykola Dzherya* and *The Kaidash Family* are studied in secondary schools in Ukraine and are familiar to anyone with this educational background.

old mother Larina and the old usurer woman,[*] but he stands up for Mother Russia!"

And so, having been involved for several years in modern and post-modern nationalist circles, he had learned to hold his own on the opposite side too, in discussions with radical patriots; goodness knows where they had come from in such numbers to occupy the Ukrainian cultural space.

"Do you want a Ukraine where flocks of cranes are flying, a Ukraine of pure morning dew? A Ukraine of biologically chaste girls and young women in traditional headwear? Do you want a patriarchal, pre-modern setup in the centre of Europe?"

"This is the only way to preserve Ukrainian uniqueness. Go to the villages! Only there can you hear the true mother tongue! Have you ever visited a simple Ukrainian village, drunk water from the well or tasted home-made bread?"

"I haven't, but I have seen them queuing in the villages to buy bread that has been delivered from elsewhere, he said, making out that the impressions of others were his own. And I know how young people from the villages are dying to move to the towns and how they want to speak Russian, so that nobody can tell they are from the country."

"Well, the village girls are still the best! And we don't want your clever-clogs, these all-too-experienced feminists in black tights, in our native Ukraine. We will boycott them!"

"You don't say! But in the offices of a certain respected newspaper I did see you offering chocolates to a lady wearing either black tights or very tight jeans."

"Young man!" The grand patriot's tone shifted from the advisory to the condescending. "What are you saying? Our conversation may be overheard by my wife! You are reducing

---

[*] i.e. the mother of Tatiana Larina, heroine of Pushkin's *Eugene Onegin*, and the elderly pawnbroker and money-lender Alyona Ivanovna murdered by Raskolnikov in Dostoevsky's *Crime and Punishment* for ideological motives. During debates on nationalism in Ukraine, Russophiles took inspiration from heroes of Russian literature.

a public debate to the level of personalities; one could even say you are stooping to gossip."

"In other words, you will boycott ladies in black tights only on a public level, but not on a personal one?"

"Don't twist my words!" said the patriot, resorting to a feeble expression someone outwitted in debate might use. "And bear in mind that you are not talking to just anyone here, but to a reputable person who has done a good deal for Ukraine!"

But notice that he doesn't ever speak Ukrainian with narrow-minded Kyivans! Some of his friends speak Ukrainian with everyone, making people struggle to find the Ukrainian words. Obviously, that is the best strategy in the case of an individualistic language policy. But in his case it did not work and he based it on his own ideology; he does not cast pearls before swine, but resolutely switches to Russian with them, even if they come up with some feeble Ukrainian linguistic formations. Ukrainian, in particular the variety spoken by his community, is the language of the intellectual aristocracy, beyond the reach of the *hoi polloi*, even if they do consider themselves patriots. Let them start speaking proper Ukrainian, not the language of Kyiv, and then he will reply to them in Ukrainian!

This is why he did not adopt his 'native tongue' when addressing those who knew him as a polite Kyiv boy who speaks Ukrainian only in class at school, because of course, as the son of a family of teachers, he was enrolled in a Ukrainian-English school, where there are traditionally fewer children from problem families. His Ukrainian language and literature teacher from the fourth to the eleventh class was a friend of his mother's, Neonila Mykytivna Bovdur. She was a typical Soviet Ukrainian teacher, dry and unimaginative; her devotion to Party and government could be seen in her eyes. She drilled her pupils strictly, making them copy out several pages from Ivan Franko's novel *Boryslav Laughs* for every Russianism they uttered verbally, and for each one in an essay or précis they had to wash the floor in the Ukrainian language classroom. And she did this not in order to educate Ukrainians in a Russified community but as a rebuff to Ukrainian bourgeois nationalists; this is how Soviet Ukrainian schoolchildren speak if you instruct them accordingly! With her, his mother adopted a comical form of Ukrainian, making insufferable errors, to which Neonila Mykytivna reacted with surprising condescension. Eugene's mother was an enthusiastic teacher of Russian language and literature. But his mother is a chapter to herself.

Oh dear! — These politicised squabbles in families, groups of friends and acquaintances! So many people fell out, and so badly that they no longer wished to see one another in the wake of such primitive altercations. And yet so many people were keen to continue these aggressive dialogues, proclaiming their vision of the future and the past of Ukraine and Russia to their obstinate interlocutors. This was the kind of endless dialogue their parents had been involved in.

"Yes, I am all for the independence of Ukraine," called out his mother. "I am opposed to Stalin! I am against the prison camps! I am against Solovki prison camp! But I am FOR Russian literature! How can you be against it? No other nation has anything like it. How can you compare Pushkin with Nechuy-Levytsky? Girls naturally much prefer Eugene Onegin to the Ukrainian classic Mykola Dzherya!"*

"Although it's much better if a girl meets an honest, hard-working fellow like Mykola Dzherya, rather than that Onegin of yours," replied father, a woodwork teacher at mother's school.

"We are not talking about that now," said mother, evading this turn the discussion was taking. "Yudushka Golovlyov — I hope to goodness you wouldn't ever come across someone like him! But what a personality! What a monster! I still can't stop shaking when I re-read how he poured vodkas for Anninka."

---

* Mykola Dzherya, the eponymous hero of a novella by the Ukrainian populist writer Ivan Nechuy-Levytsky (cf. footnote on page 25, above), is a positive figure in classical Ukrainian literature, a young villager very devoted to his wife.

"What about *Viy*, then! How can you say that isn't a monster?"

"Well, that's Gogol. He's yours and ours too."

"What do you mean, 'yours'? Are you giving up considering yourself a Ukrainian, because of Yudushka Golovlyov?"

"I am a Ukrainian who likes Russian literature! The whole world likes Russian literature, of course."

"You're exaggerating! They aren't particularly fond of it even in Russia these days." My father started telling my mother for the *n*th time about an article he had read several years ago, claiming that Moscow school-children can't distinguish Andrei Bolkonsky from Eugene Onegin.

"All the more reason why we ought not to forget the Russian classics! We will know them better than they do! Despite all the foreign literature syllabuses! That's all we need — to replace Turgenev with Salinger!"

"Well, they were quite right to replace him! I've got a Turgenev girl at home — that's enough for me!" Father embraced mother, dragging her onto the sofa, and she burst out laughing, saying that she and father had their friendly arguments. His parents were boring. He didn't even feel like arguing with them. And his mother kept shouting emotionally, as she usually did, jabbing her finger at her son.

"It's me! I was the one who got you into a Ukrainian school! Neonila Mykytivna and I made a true Ukrainian of you. Much good it has done us! You won't ever say thank you for it!"

He had disliked his own name since childhood. In every group he had belonged to as a child there had always been at least one girl called Zhenia, with whom he had been confused, for some reason, despite the fact that his surname — unlike typical Ukrainian ones — was unambiguously masculine in its grammatical form. Over the years he had repeatedly explained that his surname Samarsky was derived not from the Russian place-name Samara on the Volga, but from the name of a minor Ukrainian river, a tributary of the Dnipro. On the other hand, the Ukrainian form of Eugene's Christian name Yevheniy given him by his mother, who named him after the hero of Russian classical literature Yevgeniy Onegin, could be shortened to Yevhen to make it more masculine. That was another trump card favouring his Ukrainian conversion.

… They did not sing as a chorus until the end of the eighties. He will never forget how they sang the national anthem in the metro when it was just a song, not yet the national anthem. There were about twenty of them, roughly half lads and half girls. He put his arms round a girl's shoulders; it wasn't Lada, but she was a classy girl anyhow. She lives in Chicago these days. They meet up occasionally. Once they recalled how they used to turn people's heads in the metro; some gave them disapproving looks while others gave them looks of admiration. The latter were the majority, and some joined in and sang along with them. At the time, nobody knew how things would turn out.

"Solovki prison camp is crying its eyes out over us," said one of them, when they got tired of singing. At those words they got a fresh lease of energy and they started singing one of those Ukrainian songs that people start singing instinctively, the ones that are unstoppable, that only bullets can silence!…"

In the early nineties there was no more singing. By then it was clear that history would not be reversed, and that our national anthem would not be banned. What did ensue was poverty. Sheer poverty, at first in the form of empty shops, but then the shelves were re-filled quite quickly, though the money one managed to find somehow was only just about enough to live on modestly for a week, yet you had to survive for a month until the next pittance. Then they stopped these payments as well. Suddenly, the meaning of the crucial line of the Lord's Prayer that ran: *Give us this day our daily bread* became clear. Not when they give pay-outs in some decrepit agency where the hammer and sickle hasn't yet been replaced with the Ukrainian trident, not when someone pays for a translation for a private client, not when Lada's granny's ring is sold (it's too big for Lada's tiny finger), but *this day, this day!*

But he had a good community of friends, who helped one another to obtain orders for translation work or to write articles for a paying journal, to submit contributions to well-financed conferences, who could advise how to apply for a grant from a private foundation or a scholarship at a foreign university. So he and Lada managed to survive in those days when admission to a buffet meant that Our Father had heard the prayer and given us this day our daily bread. If they got fifty dollars for contributing to a conference, a laughable fee in international terms, the two of them were able to live decently for a month. When the money brought back from abroad paid for things you couldn't have earned enough to buy if it killed you. Alternatively, you could keep the money you brought back stashed away and you would know that even if they didn't pay you for the next six months you wouldn't die of starvation. Then something would turn up. Well, millions of fellow-citizens had no access to those conferences, those trips abroad or even to those buffets, but in those days of hyper-inflation and long-term debts incurred on the strength of his salary he felt himself far better off than in the days of boring Soviet stability. Lada occasionally went to France, he went to America. They would take off from gleaming overseas airports and land at filthy, godforsaken Boryspol, kiss on their reunion and travel into Kyiv in the darkness of night in dodgy cars, embrace on the back seat, quietly chuckling as they felt for the intimate places where the imported greenbacks were concealed.

And everything was great until Lada got pregnant. He had not expected that this event would make her so angry. She shouted, she sobbed and she uttered unmentionable words. He had already seen Lada in such a rage once before. It was the day before they decided to live together. He had a serious encounter that day with Lada and another girl as well, the one he hugged in the metro when they were singing the future national anthem in chorus. That girl was called Halya. He was slightly confused as to which girl he liked better; actually, there was also a certain charm in the idea of living with the two of them simultaneously. But he had already begun to talk with both of them about the idea that they should move in together for now and see how things went, and that put paid to the charm. Lada had an apartment on Pushkin Street, while Halya rented a studio flat in Vynohradar and would have been happy to share the payments with the young man. He was already staying overnight at both places and at both of them he had a toothbrush on the bathroom shelf.

Then one morning Lada, unable to reach him by phone at his home at Vitryani Hory, did not hesitate to go to Vynohradar and force her way into the flat rented by Halya, who was her friend as well as a classmate on a women's studies course. A fight broke out and the girls were rolling about on the floor, where blood-stains and tufts of hair soon appeared. He did his best to separate the ferocious girls, but they both pushed him away, telling him to mind his own business. Several days after this colourful brawl he moved in with Lada. And not long after that Halya went off to America.

When Lada became pregnant her aggressiveness was directed towards him. She scratched his face and tried to grab him by the hair. It was all he could do to restrain her.

"Well, after all you are twenty eight, so why not?" he said, all docile.

"What about you going round with the bulge instead of me!"

"But that's impossible! I'll be the breadwinner!"

"Clever, aren't you, you men! I suppose you'll go to a building site or get hold of some goods to sell! You'll earn money doing what you enjoy. You'll write your articles, speak at conferences, organise summer schools. While I go around with the bulge! Then I'll be in labour! Then I'll have to shove out my tits for it!"

"But it's just one child… you have to have it sometime…you said so yourself…"

"And just when I have the chance of a great women's studies placement! Any cow can give birth. But you just try writing a project that gets you selected out of a hundred applicants!"

"Not only have I tried it, but I've done it! And I'm told I have a good chance of getting a scholarship to spend a year in the States!"

"And you would be off there without me?"

"If we finally got married, you could come as well."

He didn't actually know why no doctor would give Lada an abortion at that time, which meant that her pregnancy became a harsh reality, not some vague probability. Grandfather Vasyl was the only one who accepted it positively. Grandmother Nina supported her daughter, saying she too once gave birth to Lada, complicating her life, and she still hadn't resolved matters. On top of that she is getting lumbered with a grandson, one she isn't prepared to lovingly embrace.

Normal life was over. From now on, every day was a nightmare. Madame Nebuvaiko could burst into the bedroom of the future parents to ask whether they had arranged for the move to Eugene's parents' house yet. Let them retire and look after the little one. She and Vasyl Tarasovych couldn't possibly cope with that. They had supported the young couple for some time and now it was the turn of the other side of the family. Eugene couldn't recognise his mother-in-law, who until recently had been tolerant, who hadn't ever interfered in Eugene and Lada's life; the spaciousness and convenient layout of the flat on Pushkin Street had been conducive to that. His parents in their two-room high-rise flat on the outskirts would find it much harder to be tolerant.

Eugene was beginning to seriously consider the option of escaping to his parents' place —without Lada and the child, of course. He was fed up of these rows. He needed a marriage like this like a hole in the head. Anyway, he and Lada weren't officially married, which would actually make life simpler for both of them later on. Meanwhile, a convenient incident occurred. He saw Lada in a café on the Khreshchatik with some man. As it subsequently turned out, it was Thierry. Eugene and Lada did not live in a world where a man raises merry hell if he spots his wife in a café with some bloke. But after living on Pushkin Street for a few months in an atmosphere of daily hell-raising, he crudely expressed doubts about his paternity, slammed the door behind him, dropped the key in and returned to his parents' house. He subconsciously thanked Lada's feminist leanings which meant she never wanted them to run the family finances jointly, as he took with him the greenbacks he had brought back from his trips to America.

His parents were not at all pleased at his return. They enjoyed very much living on their own in their two-room flat. The very first night at home he was awoken by their disgruntled whispering — "Quiet, I don't think he's asleep." The honeymoon was over, so to speak. In the morning they started heaping ignominy on their son:

"You rat! Running away from your pregnant wife!"

Then he said he would bring his pregnant wife home. Which immediately calmed his parents down; they were now more understanding of their son's situation. Unlike him, they took the 'he isn't our child' scenario to be a proven fact rather than something hypothetical.

"Why should we retire only to give ourselves all that hassle, fussing over your slapper Lada's child fathered by goodness knows who?"

"That's the daughters of party bosses for you! You should have found a less pretentious girl!"

"Yes, we always told you so!"

Eugene was informed of the birth of Myroslav. He went round to the house, held the baby in his arms for three minutes — it looked much the same as those that others of his age were gradually starting to have. Then grandmother Nina took the little one away and went out with him. Lada deposited a sack full of books at his feet; they must have been his, because he was disgustingly gratified.

Grandfather Vasyl named the boy Myroslav, because in Ukrainian this name meant he brought peace (*myr*) and fame (*slava*) to the family. As he and Lada were not legally married, Eugene signed the necessary papers, acknowledging the child as his and giving him his surname, so the new entry in the Ukrainian register of births read: Myroslav Evgenovych Samarsky.

But Eugene Samarsky did not return to the Nebuvaikos' home. For sure, if he had made a serious effort to care for the little one they would have taken him back at Pushkin Street. But he didn't feel like nursing the baby any more than Lada did. All the more so since he held a trump card, albeit a fake one — doubts over the paternity. Actually, he wasn't in any doubt about his paternity and he could even say exactly when it had happened, to within a week. Lada had been to France six months previously; that was where she met Thierry. But she returned to Eugene's open arms. Something might have taken place between her and Thierry at that time. But the Frenchman was in no way responsible for the birth of Myroslav.

Thierry and Lada began corresponding; he sent his letters to the main post office, to be collected as *poste restante*. This was an epistolary flirtation. Lada hadn't yet made up her mind, as everything would be decided by her trip to the feminism summer school in Belgium that Thierry was also to attend. At that time Lada was proud that she had not accepted any money from Thierry, when he had had invited her to visit him and offered to pay her fare. No, as an independent woman, she would travel to Europe if it was paid for with her own hard-earned cash, or by some organisation, but not if it was paid for by men. Then there was suddenly this pregnancy and Eugene's decision to go to America for a year. Any modern woman would go mad and lash out at a man who behaved so arrogantly. She was quite distraught, and she booked a telephone call to Thierry at that main post office. He came over and comforted her, saying that the main thing was for her to be taken care of. But he was staying put. He would have to get a divorce; unlike Lada, he was legally married.

Later on, after she and Thierry had finally sorted everything out, grandfather Vasyl said he wouldn't let them have Myroslav. They could produce French children, but Myroslav would remain Ukrainian. He and grandmother Nina were still young and they would bring up the son that Nina had been reluctant to have, after Lada.

Dad had turned so many sensible Ukrainians into informers that, following Ghandi's theory, he felt obliged to bring up at least one in a different environment.

"Was it all so serious?"

"It certainly was!" said Lada, naming one of their shared friends, and when Eugene expressed his great surprise she said she had known that young man before the great changes. But that was a quite different story; the time wasn't ripe in Ukraine to go into that yet.

"But you were always fond of your father," said Eugene, who well remembered Lada sitting on her father's lap, with her arms round his neck, burying her fingers in his hair.

"I love him now too, and I miss him," replied Lada.

"Do you miss him more than the little one?"

"What about you — who do you miss more in that America of yours? Your son or your father?" asked Lada in reply.

This conversation took place in Thierry's house in the Camargue, where they were celebrating Myroslav's fifth birthday. That was the second time Eugene had seen his son. Grandmother Nina had brought the dear chubby-cheeked lad to see his mother and his French stepfather. Nina looked rejuvenated, elegant and amicable; she had left her shrew's mask back home in Pushkin Street, hidden away somewhere in a cupboard of Soviet provenance. Grandfather Vasyl had stayed behind to look after the house. Eugene never saw him again.

Eugene had come with Dounia. By then he had received a US residence permit, so he could travel anywhere in the world. Everyone was pleased, everything was sorted out, everything was fine. Little Myroslav recited short poems in French, English and Ukrainian, to the rapturous delight of everyone present. Thierry told Eugene, in English, that his house hadn't seen such a cordial gathering since the late 17th century. Incidentally, at that time he had not yet definitively acquired legal ownership of that house from his ex-wife, Lada's predecessor, so it looked as though it would be sold. However, eventually things worked out differently for Thierry's former wife, and Lada became the legal owner of a unique example of Baroque architecture.

Everything turned out well for Eugene as well. Or almost everything. Not exactly as he wanted, but well enough. Unlike Lada, although he had come to enjoy foreign travel, he never dreamed of emigrating. But fate was to decree otherwise, so it could not be helped, even if he had displayed three times as much vital determination.

At that time, in the year his son was born, Eugene happened to experience an unfavourable phase in his life. He had no money: his savings were gradually draining away, with no prospects of their replenishment. He did not have a wife; it was all over with Lada. The other girls had long since drifted away and there were no new ones on the scene. He didn't even have anywhere to live; his parents continued to view his return home as an unfortunate misunderstanding, and somewhere to sleep only if he was at home by evening. If he returned late, he had to get either his father or his mother off the sofa which he considered his own. The only link to his former proper existence was the anticipation of a year's scholarship in America. But so far he had received no confirmation. In Kyiv, property prices had soared, so he didn't know whether he would be able to buy a flat of his own with the money brought back from America, or even whether he would be fortunate enough to receive the scholarship.

And then, out of the blue, *the uncle, a man of the most honest principles,* materialised. Or, according to the classic Ukrainian translation of the immortal Russian novel in verse, *his honest, uncle, beyond reproof.*

3. The honest uncle, beyond reproof

"You should read this letter," said his mother, holding out the envelope.

"Just read what the General writes," said his father.

It was a letter from his mother's elder brother, a colonel or lieutenant-colonel, who had retired long before the collapse of the Soviet Union and bought a house in some village, where he still lived. All Eugene could remember was that this uncle once came to stay in their house a long time ago, and he had no particular recollection of him. Except that Eugene had been put to bed on a small sofa in the kitchen, as the visitor was given his bedroom. Actually no, he didn't spend the night with them, apparently. He just visited, staying somewhere else. But for many years now greeting cards sent by him have turned up in their mailbox, on family birthdays and on former Soviet official holidays as well.

"Did you get a birthday card from the General this year too?" his father asked his mother. His parents had some connection with this uncle, but he had absolutely none at all. And now here they are suggesting he should read a letter from this man. From the *General,* as they called him.

"Read it, go on!" says his father.

My dear sister and family,
The years go by and they don't bring good health — quite the
opposite. Yesterday, before the first storm of summer, I felt so bad

I thought you would be receiving a letter written in handwriting you couldn't recognise. But we have a doctor here, Volodya — he's young, but he's very good; he's the one who brought me back to life. So I'm writing to you myself. As you know, of course, my wife died when I was still in the army. God gave us no children. I didn't re-marry, although there were plenty of interested parties, since I own a big house. In our village only the chairman of the collective farm has a bigger one. I could still get married to any pretty widow in our village even now, but since I didn't do so fifteen years ago I won't do it now, that's for sure. In your invitation to the May Day and Victory Day celebrations you wrote that Eugene was separated and was coming back to live with you. Perhaps he would come over and help me out in the last months of my life? Then I would leave my house to him. He is not the legal heir, as he is considered a distant relative. But in my will he receives everything. My house, where you have never once visited me, is a spacious, solidly built structure. Admittedly, the furniture is old, and the floorboards creak badly, but the house is well-built, the roof doesn't leak, and there is a big loft and a very good cellar. There are two storehouses outside as well.
I don't know, of course, whether perhaps Eugene is unable to come here, because he has a job. Let me know if Eugene won't be coming, in which case I will look for other options.

"There is a toilet in this big house, is there?" enquired Eugene.

"At the moment it's summer, so that isn't so important."

"Won't he last till the winter, then?"

"Well, perhaps there is a toilet. I think he said there was."

"There's a sauna at any rate. He once invited me to come over for a sauna," Dad recalled.

"Saunas are usually in an outbuilding, I think." Eugene recalled the local government summer school, financed by the US State Department and based at the Soviet Communist Party sanatorium near Kyiv, where they had a sauna in a separate building. Those were the days!"

"Do go, in any case! For an army man to have written such a long letter means he must be in a bad way!"

"This house will sell, even without a toilet."

"Go there while the weather is still fine," trilled Mother.

"Go on, he might snuff it and the house would go to the collective farm," Dad put in his bit.

"Seems you're kicking me out!" he shouted at his parents.

"Go back to your mother-in-law's then!"

"Take the kid for a walk!"

"Give him a bath!"

"Change his nappies!"

"They have Pampers now!" retorted Eugene.

"So much the better! Go back to your child!"

"That's where you belong!"

"You've acknowledged him, haven't you? So you know very well he's yours!"

"So why are you sitting around here, miles away from your child?"

"Doing your parents' heads in!"

"We brought you up; we didn't dump you on your grandparents!"

"And you give us no peace in our old age!

But if you don't want to look after your child, go to the village."

"There's nothing to keep you in Kyiv, anyway; you just sit around in some coffee-house on the Khreshchatik!"

The fact that his useless parents, who very rarely made it to Kyiv city centre, knew he was accustomed to sitting for ages on a tall stool by the window in a coffee-house, known unofficially as *The Tube*, only occasionally taking his eyes off some book, just went to show that Kyiv was one big village. He really did need to escape from here. But not to some village, for God's sake!...

There really was no longer anything to keep Eugene in Kyiv. He continued to belong to an organisation that was no longer functioning, one where the employees went just to collect their wages. But they had stopped paying them, so there was no point in going there at all. Besides, since he had broken up with Lada he hadn't had any luck with the casual jobs he used to be inundated with, giving him more work than he could cope with, so that he sometimes had to share it out. Of course, the majority of his clients used to contact him by phone at Pushkin Street. He had carried out the work pretty well, but it was not very demanding. So the clients wouldn't have shifted heaven and earth to seek him out. Most likely, they were looking for an alternative translator.

Besides, decent Ukrainian society was gradually beginning to re-organise itself. Nobody fell out with anybody, but they found better, more important, things to do than spending time together. Some found means of earning good money, some went abroad, some settled down with their families. Probably, that spring he was the only one who experienced a resurgence of energy driving him to seek the company of others. Probably, that spring the reserves of energy that drove him to seek the company of others were revived. However, this was rather out of a lack of anywhere to go than out of any burgeoning youthful energy.

Eugene had not expected to inherit from his *honest uncle, beyond reproof.* A common topic of conversation among their circle of acquaintances was a girl who had undertaken to look after her lonely teacher in return for inheriting her house. The teacher had not died yet — it was three years now — and she just tormented her carer, declaring that the girl paid her no attention and that she was just waiting for her to die. So the unfortunate carer (*the sitter*, as she was jokingly nicknamed) was considering tearing up their agreement.

Eugene decided to move to the village anyhow. After all, why not go for a stroll in the country, not entertaining any particular expectations, while the weather was fine? He had been to a pig-farm in America, where they took them on an excursion because the sponsor of the *Public Service Journalists* programme was the leading pig farmer in the region. So why not drop in on a Ukrainian village where Eugene Samarsky had never been before? After all, that was where *the source of Ukrainian speech and spirituality* was to be found — naturally, he uttered these words with an ironic intonation, but he could not find any other way of expressing something like that, and he did not try anyway.

His uncle wrote that the village was a two-hour train journey from Kyiv, getting off at Irivka—Kobivka station. Then it was a five kilometre walk to Irivka. Perhaps someone would pick him up on the way and give him a lift on their cart.

Eugene set off without more ado. If everything turned out as his *honest uncle, beyond reproof* wrote, he would go back home for his suitcase. That uncle in Russian classical literature snuffed it before his heir arrived. The young wastrel received the inheritance, however. First of all, though, he would have to *give assurance of his respect*. How many months would he have to give it for? Until autumn? Until winter? Or, like their *sitter* friend, indefinitely?

He got off at the designated station, binning the *Man and Woman* adult magazine which he had bought for some reason from a disabled person on the train. A woman carrying two large baskets joined together by some twisted old head-scarf got off too. He was just thinking that he ought to give the woman a hand with lifting this heavy burden when she deftly threw the baskets over her shoulder, one on her back, the other in front, and set off smartly towards the dilapidated steps leading from the platform to the scarcely discernible footpath through the grass. In all directions there stretched fields full of flowers and somewhere on the horizon dark streaks of some sort could be seen; it was probably the forest. There were no buildings to right or left of the track, so the IRIVKA KOBIVKA sign on the platform — the last two letters had fallen off — was like something off the set of a drama of the absurd.

The woman with the two baskets was moving on quickly; at any moment she would disappear into the long grass. There was nobody else on the platform. He would have to stop her somehow and ask where Irivka was, as there would be nobody else. The next train was due here in three hours' time. Eugene was overcome with a sense of cosmic helplessness on the deserted station in the middle of the endless, flourishing plain — once an elderly traditional patriot explained to him, adopting an air of superiority, that fields, steppe, and meadows were quite different things, which a good Ukrainian should not confuse.

"Prairie, pampas, savannah," he said, continuing the semantic series.

And now he was standing God knows where, not knowing which way to go. There was no returning home, of course, as otherwise it would have been better not to go in the first place. But while he was consulting the tinny train timetable board, the woman with the baskets would disappear, and it was certain that another one would not come along. So he had better catch her up.

"Excuse me, Madam!"

The woman carried on, paying no attention to his shouting. She had evidently never expected to be addressed as *madam*. Somehow he had not felt he could address her, as they do in Kyiv, as *Woman*! Suddenly he remembered an expression from some stage performance:

"My good woman! Stay a while!"

The woman turned round:

"What do you want, son?"

"Er, how do I get to Irivka?"

This path here takes you straight to Irivka. But don't follow it, son. It's very dewy. Go that way, towards yonder post — see it? Over there's the road to Irivka. Follow it, and turn left when you get to the big oak tree. Then there'll be somebody you can ask.

He took a few steps along the footpath, as he didn't want to let the only person around out of his sight. But his feet suddenly felt wet, as though he had been wandering around in the rain for a long time. He decided that the warning not to go this way because it was "very dewy" made sense. So he turned back and set off in the direction the woman had shown him. He reached the post, and saw a wide, dusty track which ran perpendicular to the railway line. The optical laws in this rural environment are strange. If you look straight along this path, you can see low white-brick buildings with painted wooden verandas, which were quite invisible from the path across the field.

"I'm in a village, I'm in a Ukrainian village for the first time in my life," he realised as he walked along the track.

Here he began to come across some people. Occasionally he was overtaken on the track by cyclists, and now out of the blue a cart appeared, drawn by a chestnut horse with a black tail. No cars, he thought. The cyclists rapidly disappeared, but the cart drove alongside him for some time.

"Am I going the right way for Irivka?" he asked the old man driving the cart.

"If you aren't scared of getting your trousers mucky, get on," said the man.

After a while, the old man mentioned that Irivka was slightly out of his way — he was going to Kobivka, but from Kobivka to Irivka it was just a stone's throw. The old man repeated this information several times. Eugene just nodded.

By the big oak he was ready to get off, but the old man said he wanted the part of Irivka that was closer to the field, so it would be more convenient to go via Kobivka. When he asked the old man how he knew where he was going, the reply came:

"Well, you're going to the General's, aren't you?"

To this day he doesn't know where the old man on the cart got his information from, but his sources were correct.

"He may be a colonel to you, but to us he's the General," he said, shortly reining in the horse, so Eugene could easily get off. "And now, see them three birches? Just past there is the turning into the General's place."

No sooner had he reached the three birches than a woman in a blindingly white head-scarf appeared out of nowhere and called out to him:

"This way! The General is expecting you."

He was no longer surprised by the rural tom-toms. But as he was walking from the three birches to the grey-brick house pointed out to him by the woman with the white scarf, it occurred to him: this is it, Ukraine. Here they have always spoken Ukrainian. Even in the days when I was a pupil at a Ukrainian school, but spoke Russian outside school, as everybody else did, and when I studied in Russian at university, and when I started speaking Ukrainian during the great changes. Here Ukrainian has always been the natural form of speech, without any self-awareness or any ideas of nationalism or patriotism. Those who moved away from here into the towns converted to Russian; they had to suffer the cramped conditions of filthy communal living quarters and the extortionate costs of rotten rented flats, but having to forget their native language wasn't a problem at all. Those who stayed here effortlessly use words which I often have to spend ages searching for in dictionaries.

His first impression of this house was that it was definitely the General's. Single-storey, but tall. A steep roof — the ceilings must be high in the rooms; look how tall the windows are, and they are high above ground level. Eugene recognised details the General had mentioned in his letter: solid foundations, a good loft. In the bright blue sky above the house, swallows with shining white bellies were swooping wildly. Above one of the windows of the General's house was a swallow's nest, from which several wide-open beaks protruded.

"Yesterday one wee swallow chick fell from the nest," said the woman standing at the entrance to the General's land, realising what he was looking at. She stood at his side, having materialised again out of nowhere.

"Just go in, he's waiting for you," went on the woman. "The entrance is on the other side. Follow the house around and go in. The latch is stiff — give it a good jerk."

Sure enough, the latch was pretty stiffish. And the floor in the General's house really did creak badly. Eugene, like everybody else in the village, was already thinking of his relative as the General, rather than as his *honest uncle, beyond reproof.* This is amazing! Beyond the large kitchen one large empty room after another. Only when he reached the third one did he find the old man, sitting in a leather armchair with wooden armrests, next to a table.

The General spoke in Russian. What is more, just like his sister, that is to say Eugene's mother, he talked in lines from Russian classical literature. To tell the truth, however, he was quite unlike his sister, since apart from a few commonplaces he knew nothing. Of Pushkin's immortal work, which his mother knew off by heart virtually in its entirety, he knew only the first four lines about the *honest uncle* who demanded to be *respected.*

"Well, do you respect me, Zhenia?" asked the General, with the laugh of a stroke patient.

Eugene shrugged his shoulders.

"I've no reason not to respect you."

"But there's no reason to respect me either."

"I am accustomed to take respect for granted."

"That is very sensible of you."

They conversed in Russian. That day and the following days as well. The General always responded to his fellow-villagers in Ukrainian though. In Irivka they spoke good Ukrainian and you heard Ukrainian-Russian hybrid speech only when it came to words which were alien to the rural way of life. The General had also picked up good Ukrainian from the villagers. But with his nephew, who he evidently considered a representative of his own world, he conversed in Russian. This happened of its own accord; there were no conscious motivations involved. Eugene did not ask the General why he had become bilingual in the village, rather than converting completely to Ukrainian, the language everyone spoke round here. Instead, he asked how he came to choose this particular house in the village when he retired.

"Because it was the only opportunity to live in a big house. In town they offered me a one-room flat. In a good house, in the centre of the chief town of the region, but just the one room. My wife died of cancer two years before my retirement. It was my fault — I once made her have an abortion, because at the beginning of my army career we lived in terrible conditions. I expected everything to sort itself out later and I thought we would have children. But it didn't work out; after that she was ill all her life. For other women it turned out all right, but not for her. I had ideas about re-marrying and making a new wife happy, bringing my princess to the big house. In our regiment there was a lieutenant from this village; he visits occasionally — he's a major now. He told me about this house. I bought it from the local council, not from private owners. I got permission — in those days you had to get permission for everything. But I didn't get married again after all. It didn't work out. I courted my wife for a year before we started going out together. This time all the young widows in the village started bringing me apples, honey and milk, they were keen to dig over my garden, when I still had one, to tidy up in the house and beat the carpets. Not only widows, actually, but even unmarried girls. For several years I worked at the local school as a military training officer. There are some excellent girls here — I bequeath them all to you. Your mother wrote that you used to be married to the daughter of a Soviet bigshot."

"There was even a child."

"But the child isn't yours, is it?"

"Mother was very forthcoming in her letters to you, evidently."

"She just added two or three lines to the Victory Day greetings."

Eugene liked living in the General's house. He moved into the other wing. His bedroom was far from that of his *honest uncle, beyond reproof*; he was not ever asked to re-arrange the sick man's pillows at night.

Eugene went back home briefly for his things. He brought a pile of books. Some of them were a gift from old Mme Nebuvaiko. He was delighted to take with him the bag full of books Lada had returned to him when he came to see the little one. Amongst them there was even the famous two-volume work by Nietzsche with a black cover, published during the *perestroika* period, but previously he hadn't had time to read these books carefully. Actually, he had acquired the knack of including quotations from them in his articles without delving deeply into the immortal texts. Now he could already see himself in his room, sitting at his desk next to the green lamp, attentively reading a book by Francis Bacon, for example. Or Nietzsche, that's it, Nietzsche, *The Birth of Tragedy from the Spirit of Music*! To absorb these wild ideas you need the true isolation that he would at last now enjoy. And he would continue to learn German! That's a good thing too! The darker phases of life have a deeper meaning and are much more fruitful than the brighter ones!

Eugene had returned to Kyiv only briefly. He packed his belongings and his books, and went to his mother's to pick up the CD player he had brought for her from America — she only listened to her crackly vinyl records. And then he set off back to Irivka. He arranged in advance for the old man to meet him off the morning train with his cart and take him to the General's house. The old man didn't let him down; he was waiting by the platform. He helped him to load his bags onto the cart and commanded the horse: "Gee-up!" Like Pushkin, I'm off to the great house with a cart-load of books, thought Eugene.

On the drive in front of the General's house there stood an ancient *Volga* with a metallic deer on the bonnet — the former symbol of Soviet affluence, beyond the reach of many. The car was in working order. One day Eugene and the General got in that *Volga* and drove to a nearby town.

"Is it all right for you to drive?" asked Eugene, alarmed.

"Just let any policeman try stopping the General's car!" his uncle replied. "We won't drive on the main road; mind you, they themselves can get away with driving around here drunk, in the nude and without number plates."

In town they arranged their affairs through a notary, and Eugene obtained the certificate, signed and sealed, giving him inheritance rights.

"I don't know how to thank you," muttered Eugene on the return journey, because he had to say something. "It's a shame my parents have never been to see you."

"Now you are the most eligible bachelor in all Irivka," laughed the General. "You'll see that I'm not just leaving you a big house, I'm leaving you the entire village."

The General turned out to be indeed *his honest uncle, beyond reproof.* The very next day after their trip to the district council he was taken ill. Volodya, the doctor from the local health centre, hurried round and stayed with him for several hours, while Eugene sat in the north wing at the desk by the green glass lamp which he had taken from the General's table. Then Volodya solemnly summoned him. Eugene was overwhelmed, not only by the death as such, but because it felt as if he had come here merely to inherit. During these few weeks he had become attached to the General and he had become very involved in the sad story of his life. He felt great sadness when Volodya led him to the General's bedroom, so that, in accordance with some local custom, Eugene himself could fold the General's arms across his chest. *And centuries-old notions, And fateful mysteries of death...* Eugene sat on a chair at his dead uncle's bedside, while Volodya went to the front room to complete the General's death certificate. It was four o'clock on a summer's morning and dawn was breaking. Outside the window, the voices of the village women could be heard, getting louder and louder. Goodness knows how, they had already found out all about it.

All the villagers recognised Eugene as the General's sole legal heir. As his next of kin, he solemnly took the long, slow walk directly behind the hearse, and the whole village followed behind.

But not everything was so straightforward. In the course of the funeral supper it was revealed that the General had actually re-married. And he was not divorced. His second wife, a young librarian employed by the district council, had lived in his house for a short time. She left him back in Soviet times, helping herself to his late first wife's gold jewellery, and several hundred Soviet roubles in cash which the General had withdrawn from his savings account at her request because she said her mother needed help. After Ukrainian independence, this petty swindler never re-appeared. When you take a long time to make a choice and you are too fastidious, you are bound to make a wrong decision, as was the case with the General. So, as the notary officially informed Eugene, he would have to wait for six months after the General's death before he could inherit. If the swindler did not turn up within six months, he could inherit the house and do what he liked with it. If she turned up, it would not all be so straightforward for her either. But she could apply to the court, and if she found a decent lawyer she would probably be awarded a share in the house. But nobody was going to actively search for the General's wife, now his widow.

"The Muscovite!" the women at the wake called her. "They sent her to our district from the Saratov Region.

"What's this?" wondered Eugene. "A special sort of patriotism? Or a primitive sense of otherness?"

His parents did not come to the funeral, although he sent them a telegram from the local post office, where they opened up especially for him, since the General had not died on a weekday. After the funeral Eugene went home, to bring his parents over for the commemoration dinner on the ninth day. Father and mother debated for a long time whether they should go or not. It was rather awkward to go to pay your respects when you hadn't ever been to see him when he was alive, his father said. Mother shilly-shallied for a long time, then she also decided not to go.

She tipped out a pile of old photographs on the floor and found several pictures of her elder brother. She recalled how proud she had felt as a seven year old girl on the one or two occasions when her elder brother, a military cadet, collected her from school. She found a wedding photograph of the late General. His young wife was remarkably beautiful. Or perhaps it was just a particularly good photograph? Mother said she would be thinking of her brother at home, rather than in the company of the village women, who she didn't know. But she would allow Eugene to say she had been taken ill, and actually she did have great difficulty in breathing! So he told his new neighbours how seriously ill his mother was and that his father was unable to leave her and the women sighed in sympathy.

In the house of his late uncle, Eugene found the same photograph which his mother had shown him, and many more besides. Unlike his mother's photographs, the General's archive was organised in military fashion. All the photographs were in albums, in strict chronological order with the dates written in pencil. The General's first wife was very beautiful in other photographs as well, taken when she was older. As the General's heir, Eugene felt justified in placing a photograph of this woman who had died a long time ago on the table in his wing. There was no photograph of the district librarian in the General's archive, however. Eugene spent several days delving into someone else's life, sorting out old documents and belongings. He was gradually entering a different dimension, one in which he had never lived, and the incredible silence of his uncle's (now actually his own) house with its high ceilings and creaky floorboards conjured up certain weird sensations which he had not previously experienced.

But his day-to-day concerns kept driving these weird sensations out of his mind. Eugene went down into a cellar — not the one adjacent to the house, which was full of old potatoes beginning to go to seed, but the one under the house. Military orderliness ruled there too. Bottles of alcohol stood in rows on the shelves like soldiers on parade. Mostly Soviet brands of cognac. There were also countless jars of pickled gherkins, tomatoes, mushrooms, various salads and seasoned tomatoes. It is unlikely that the General had filled these one-litre and three-litre jars himself. Most probably, they had been brought to him in the summer and autumn by women from the village.

All the drawers in the General's desk were full of exercise books containing his notes. The General had attempted to make sense of his life, assiduously recording events which were especially relevant to him. Perhaps the main reason for leaving the house to his nephew, a university graduate — and the General might not have realised it himself — was that someone would read the uncle's notes and find a way of turning them into someone's legacy, albeit their own. So that the reams of paper containing his writings over so many years would not end up in the stove, since in Irivka, where in winter they burned wood, the papers would naturally find their way into the fire, as naturally as spring follows winter. One day, Eugene decided to delve into this archive. He might find something in it. But he put off this irksome task until better times.

For the time being, he laid Nietzsche's two-volume work on the table in the north wing, together with Milan Kundera's *Immortality*, a two-volume work by Francis Bacon and several issues of the Ukrainian contemporary affairs journal *Suchasnist*. And also a bilingual edition of *Eugene Onegin* comprising the original and a Ukrainian translation, which he had bought for ten coupons from some old lady in the Kyiv flea market. He inserted the *Egmont Overture* disc into the CD player. It was impossible to read to Beethoven. To Vivaldi or Mozart you could read, write, and eat, even though they are great composers. But they are not so jealous; you don't have to commit yourself to them totally, whereas Beethoven was probably the first to disallow this. If you ate while listening to Beethoven, you were sure to start feeling sick. On the other hand, while listening to Beethoven, as is the case with other great German composers, you could easily engage in some physical activity such as tidying the house or moving furniture around, which he started doing while *Egmont* was on. Eugene decided to note down this little 'musicological' discovery, but he would do it some other time.

4. The village where Eugene was bored

Eugene was not bored in the village.

He did not live the life of a villager. He did not dig the garden, he did not go haymaking, he had no chickens, ducks or turkeys to feed, he had no cows to milk and he didn't have to queue up for bread. However, at home he had vegetables and bread, and something to spread on it. So his way of life could be categorised as that of a gentleman of leisure. But he did not enjoy the way his life had turned out in his uncle's house. In the morning they would bring him milk, which he didn't drink, as "our home-produced milk, straight from the cow, not what you get in the town" made him feel violently sick. So he used to pass on the milk to another woman, the one who brought him vegetables; once, she brought him a chicken. The 'vegetable' woman didn't have a cow, and she was glad of this exchange in kind. But the one who brought the milk learned of its fate and she reacted in a rather strange way. She did not stop bringing her unwanted product; instead, on her next visit she emptied her litre jug into an enormous glass and said to Eugene:

"Just get this down you straight away, while I watch! You turn your nose up at it because you've never drunk home-produced milk."

He had to come out with some nonsense about having suffered from an allergy to milk as a child, which in adulthood had developed into some even worse affliction. So milk was a no-no. His mother had once bought fresh milk for him from a woman in the village, but it made him more ill than that bought in the shop.

"You are starving in the town! You are not getting paid! So be glad you are in the village and that everything is provided," said She who brings the milk, defending her position — as Eugene described her way of thinking.

"Folk are poor in the town," said another of his suppliers, the Vegetable Woman, in her support. "They pay for things that we find lying about at our feet."

"What's more, they spend over three quarters of their income on them," said Eugene, in defence of their rural pride. "But why do you bring me cabbages and carrots? You could sell them at the market, you know!"

"I'd sooner bury them than sell them for the hundred thousand I get for them in town," said the Vegetable Woman, offended.

At that time, denominations of hundreds of thousands and millions were in circulation. Eugene left Ukraine before the *hryvna* was introduced. Since they brought it in after he had left, it was a long time before he even saw the currency some patriots were so proud of.

But at that time the hundreds of thousands of coupons were spent very economically. In the uncle's cellar there were lots of old potatoes, which shortly before his arrival the neighbours had transferred into dry boxes. So he had enough to boil or fry for his dinner until September, until they dug up some more. There were his uncle's preserves from the cellar as well. But there were also salads from the fresh heads of cabbages which the women brought him, covered in drops of dew. But it demanded a lot of effort, sometimes superhuman efforts, to stop them chopping up the salad in his own kitchen.

These women ruled his life. They came one after another, so many that he couldn't remember their names, entering his house without knocking, bringing cabbages and carrots, speck and eggs, cows' milk and goats' milk, as though to the altar of some pagan god, whose role he did not want to assume. The *honest uncle, beyond reproof* had left him a heavy legacy, and actually he had honestly forewarned him of it.

The women told him there wouldn't be any tomatoes that year, but there would be enough cucumbers and marrows. They said a coypu had gnawed through the wire mesh of the cage at the head teacher's and escaped, while the two rabbits belonging to the deputy head had died, so it wasn't certain whether she would have enough fur to make a fur coat, though unfortunately she had already come to an arrangement with the furrier. They said that the director of the collective farm had ordered all the Irivka secondary school teachers to weed twenty rows of beetroot each, justifying himself by saying that they always came to the collective farm for help when they needed it. Eugene's women, the majority of whom were teachers themselves, were incensed at the decision of the collective farm administration. They said that when their children were old enough they would be taking them to school, not to the collective farm. The women also said there was a new foreign language teacher, the woman who was trying to sit next to you at the wake, on your right, do you remember, Zhenia?

"Sitting next to me there was some talkative woman with a fine head of grey hair…"

"That's the head teacher at our school, Hanna Petrivna; what, don't you know her yet, Zhenia?"

"I admit that I don't."

"And you know that new English woman, the rather sexy one who came to the wake in a low-cut dress, well, she went all the way to Kyiv yesterday to have an abortion! And now Hanna Petrivna doesn't know how she can keep her on in her job at the school."

"Hasn't Hanna Petrivna ever had an abortion then?"

"God forbid, Zhenia! Hanna Petrivna is married! Her husband is an inspector with the traffic police. She has two sons, and the elder one is getting married in the autumn. And this Angela… what's her name… is only in her first year with us. What will happen now? If she is dismissed, where will we find another English teacher?"

If the Irivka women limited themselves to passing on the village news, one could stomach that somehow. But they wanted greater recompense for their gifts. They wanted to know his every step, at least within the bounds of the General's house, which, according to some quaint decrees, they considered their common property.

"How did you sleep last night? Did you hear what I said? How did you sleep?"

He had to mutter something; otherwise the Irivka woman would keep repeating her enquiry again and again. In response to his "Well, I slept rather badly; there were thunderclaps, but it didn't actually rain" she recounted how she had slept badly too, then she had fallen asleep in the small hours and had a dream about a wedding in the General's house, and the table was laid in the garden, although the late General had sawn up all the tables and benches and even dug up all the wooden posts, and black birds were circling above the young couple, but they were not crows, they were enormous birds of some sort, like eagles… Her eyes were wide and bulging as she retold the dream, and the tone of her voice was like something from a horror film.

One day he was brought a basket of early-ripened apples by a very young girl. He was struck not so much by her beauty, although she was certainly a very attractive little thing, as by a certain naïve directness, verging on idiocy. This child, unlike the other young Irivka women, rushed into the kitchen. The older women would hurriedly pass through the kitchen and the sitting room, rushing into the study and the bedroom, and if he was not to be found in his uncle's south wing they went looking for him in the north wing. But this young girl shifted from one foot to another, waiting for him to emerge and holding the rather heavy basket with both hands.

"What can I do for you, my dear?" he asked.

The girl offered him the basket of apples and he thanked her for this further gift. She asked if she might have a look round. He gave her a brief tour of the General's house and she asked how many square metres this and that room measured, noted that there were two stoves, and regretted that although there was a toilet inside the house it was out of order. Well, to repair the sewerage system he would have to call for a qualified plumber, as a village handyman would not manage it. And it would not come cheap.

On the bottom shelf of the sideboard there stood a large soup tureen belonging to an English dinner service his uncle had been given as a retirement present. This was where Eugene put the apples the girl had brought; for sure, nobody had ever used it for soup. He had never come across such fragrant, sweet early-ripening apples before.

Volodya sometimes visited him in the evening. He was the only person in Irivka he was pleased to see. They sat at the round table; he opened the glass doors of the sideboard to take out crystal glasses and one of his uncle's cognacs. He found Volodya's physical presence quite congenial. He liked to observe the doctor's youthful features and to hear him talk, although Volodya rarely expressed an original thought. On one occasion Eugene attempted to discuss the topic of nationalism with him, but he got no reaction:

"Well, what if I am called out to Tykhonovych — God forbid — am I not supposed to help him?" Tykhonovych was some Russian who had moved to their village because he married a local woman, and he was a 'good Russian man'.

"Oh no, that's not what I mean at all," said Eugene, noting Volodya's naivety about nationalism; however, he still found him pleasant company.

Volodya came round the evening of the day when the girl had visited in the morning.

"They've got some sort of Michurin apple tree, unique in the village," confirmed Volodya, who somehow knew who the girl was that called on Eugene.

"Tell me, why are they eating apples a month before the Feast of the Transfiguration?" asked Eugene, all of a sudden demonstrating a knowledge of rural rituals.

"Well, who knows those rules these days? When they opened the Church of St. Panteleimon here, the teachers didn't know which hand to cross themselves with! My mother showed those women how to do it; she had never been a Party member, you see. As for those apples, you have to eat them as soon as possible, because if you leave them for a while they get just as bitter as the rest of them. This is a heathen apple tree, you could say. They know this, and they keep giving them away to everybody," laughed Volodya. He went on to explain that knowledge of the local mythology was very useful to him in his work as a rural doctor. This local mythology had been preserved in Irivka, and in neighbouring Kobivka as well, under the previous regime, because the old government, unlike their treatment of the church, did not frown on rituals concerning the giving away of apples, or the folding of a deceased person's arms across the chest. Even the communists in the village adhered to local superstitions.

"You're drinking cognac from a small goblet, not moonshine from a tumbler."

"Well, I can drink moonshine if it's offered... It all depends what other people are drinking."

"But what do you prefer?"

"Your late uncle asked me that too. If there are just the two of you sitting together, cognac is better. If you are mingling in a crowd, moonshine is better."

That day — he thought of it as the day of the July apples — Eugene told Volodya sincerely how impressed he was with his discretion. He said he didn't interfere in other people's business, only crossing someone's threshold when he was welcome. Eugene would never forget how he had once started intensively reading the heart-rending lines of *The Antichrist* and Volodya, sensing the strange mood the new owner of the house was in, said he would come round again some other time. That was so different from the way the women behaved every morning, giving him no respite. Volodya was embarrassed and, unlike the girl that morning, he blushed.

"All the men are like that here," said the young doctor, "whereas the women are very assertive."

Then Eugene told Volodya all about the early-morning forays by the Irivka women into his house. About the cabbage they insisted on chopping up for him, and about the milk, and about how the women always wanted to know how he had slept last night.

"Well, let me tell you something! Has any man ever brought you carrots or a lump of lard? It's always the women. They're all the same in Irivka. They dominate the men and tell them what to do. And they treat you like a child, Zhenia!"

They probably treated the late General as a child as well. His marriage to the district librarian, a *Muscovite* at that, was something of a rebellion by a scolded child against a bevy of ferocious nannies. Nothing good came of it either, and the nannies howled in chorus: "See what you get when you don't do what sensible women tell you!"

So Eugene, as best he could, began to contest the child status which he had unexpectedly acquired in this village, and it wasn't an easy struggle. One day he locked the door, and in the morning his delivery women yanked at the door, yelling outside, while he slowly made Turkish coffee in a copper coffee-pot brought from home, patiently watching the foam oozing up to the brim of the pot. The water in the Irivka wells was actually so bitter-tasting that even strong tea could not disguise it and coffee was the only answer. This spring water, mother's holy well, tasted bitter too. However, in Kobivka, as they told him, the water was quite different. But you can't keep fetching your water from Kobivka to Irivka. At the village shop he bought cartons of juice which the sales assistant Lida handed to him over the heads of the people queuing for bread, and he brewed coffee from the well water. And then a key grated in the lock and the door opened!

"Oh my goodness, you're here!"

"Alive and kicking!"

"Didn't you hear us trying to break into the house?"

"We rushed round to Vasylivna's, because the General, God rest his soul, gave her a key when he got poorly."

"You must have heard us!"

"I had some music playing," said Eugene, making an excuse instead of firmly, not to say sharply, telling them he was not keen to see early visitors who would then roam about his house all morning.

"Well, we'll let you off this once, but from now on please don't lock up."

"We all nearly had heart failure!"

"Oh what a lovely smell! You're making coffee. In return for making us run round to Vasylivna's!"

And the women started rummaging in the General's sideboard for coffee cups.

He decided to go for morning walks in the forest, because he couldn't follow his intellectual pursuits until the evening anyway. The women drew him off course, insisting that he accepted their vegetables and spent a short while at least telling them how he had slept. And listening to the village news. The Irivka women could not contemplate the thought that they were unwelcome. Once he was finally alone, he cursed his weakness, his pitiful inability to tell them to go to hell. This annoyance troubled him all day, preventing him reading the books he had brought from home, as he needed peace and quiet to read Nietzsche or even Francis Bacon. The big isolated house at the edge of the village was perfectly suited to intensive reading. But, for some reason, his everyday village life was reminiscent of the absurd, even more so than the situation in his parents' house. When he went into the forest, if he actually managed to reach the forest, he heard voices behind him:

"If only he was going there to pick berries or gather mushrooms, but he goes there just for the sake of it. And we bring him his milk, don't we?"

"As we used to bring the General's."

"Now then, the General, what a man he was! But this one! Well, never thanks you properly!"

I don't want this sort of Ukraine," he thought. I can understand people escaping from here and doing whatever it takes to be able to afford the rent for a studio flat on the outskirts of Kyiv, as many of my acquaintances did. It is not the lack of hot running water that drives them away. They are escaping from Her who brings the milk, from Her who peeps through a gap in the fence and tells others what she has seen. From Her who brings vegetables and eggs to pay for her God-given right to peep.

Then he returned indoors and sat down at his desk to open *Thus Spoke Zarathustra*. He read that you need chaos in your soul to give birth to a dancing star. And he felt that his soul was full of some pig-swill, not even worthy to be called chaos.

As always in this stupid world, help came from a lie, not from a rope stretched across an abyss, not from a will to live. One day he told them he could go home and wait in the town until his right to inherit was confirmed. But his flat in Kyiv was too small, so his ailing parents were an encumbrance, though they didn't want to be. The thing was, he was writing his dissertation; he opened the door from the kitchen to the north sitting room wider to show the Irivka women the typewriter on his desk, which then convinced them that he actually was working on something very important, something beyond their understanding.

"So you'll be a professor?" asked the Vegetable Woman.

"I'll have a higher degree, but a professor is a university teacher."

"My son is a student at the university in Kyiv. I think he is intending to write a dissertation as well," said She who brings the milk, proudly.

"If you are writing a dissertation, you have to have quiet in the house, because the slightest sound breaks your concentration," explained Eugene.

"But you have to cook!"

"When I'm cooking a meal I carry on thinking about what I have written or what I have read."

"What's the topic of your dissertation?" enquired Halyna Dmytrivna, the surprisingly knowledgeable deputy head.

"Gender analysis of everyday cultural practice in post-Soviet society," he said, without blinking an eyelid.

"Oh, what's gender analysis?" asked She who brings the milk, incredulously.

"When I graduate I'll give you a copy of the author's summary, without fail. That will explain the whole thing quite clearly," he replied, and the women were very pleased; they left the General's house, pressing their fingers to their lips: "Shhh!"

But the following day they still came round. Then he took a desperate step, offering them payment for their produce. He didn't have much money, and he anticipated that they would refuse. And so it was. They said they would bury the vegetables anyway, so why shouldn't they feed the future holder of a higher degree?

Gradually, the women stopped annoying him. For one thing, they stopped coming so often, and for another he became accustomed to them, learning to shut out their nattering and replying in words of one syllable, telling them he was considering the next chapter of his dissertation.

Wasted days were followed by quiet evenings. Dogs barked in the distance, occasionally a bird screeched in alarm, and he thought this was somehow associated with his thought process, which simultaneously tormented and comforted him. He thought about everything on earth. He thought about the people his destiny had brought him together with. He thought about Lada, with whom he had shared so many incredible minutes, hours, days, months, but it was all in the past, and he recalled her calmly, without emotion, with no feelings of guilt or anger, unfeelingly in fact! He thought about his son Myroslav. People attach so much meaning to their children; they want so badly to have them. He had nothing against that. Yet he had fathered a son without this arousing any feelings in him. When he thought about the child he was expecting in a detached way before, he was prepared to selflessly help the woman who would give birth to it. But the child was somewhere on Pushkin Street and he was here in the village, a hundred kilometres away. What happened, happened. *We have what we have*: the aphorism of the first president of independent Ukraine came to mind, and for a moment the level of his reflections, which he was attempting to raise to the heights of a rarefied mountain atmosphere, painfully declined.

That summer in the night-time quiet of the General's house it seemed that of all things in the world what he had wanted most of all and still wanted was strong feelings, on the model of those which caused the death of Semele, mother of Dionysius, who wanted Zeus to come to her in the same splendid attire he wore for Hera. But the nymph could not survive what the goddess endured, and she died. He did not want to die, but he wanted to understand the nature of those emotions that take you to the brink of death, to the point of losing one's reason. But he did not know what he had to do in order to admit such feelings into his soul. He could only analyse his own experience. So he carefully recalled and re-lived those events which in recent years had aroused powerful emotions in him. Concentrating on his past, he admitted that his being had been overflowing with emotions when the opportunity of a new foreign journey began to dawn. He was quite unable to work as his heart pounded at the growing probability of this trip materialising. At the same time, he was conscious of having survived the break-up with Halya, with whom he had also enjoyed happy times, who Lada had beaten so relentlessly; but then Lada had been repaid too, because he could feel the place where Halya had bitten her on the shoulder for a long time afterwards. He recalled how six months later he and Lada had calmly attended the farewell dinner Halya laid on before her departure for the United States, how they took turns to kiss her. What was that about? An ability to behave correctly towards others? Or an inability to have genuine feelings?

What a powerful surge of emotions he had experienced when he began speaking Ukrainian! And however insignificant the main reasons for it were, it was through the medium of Ukrainian that he experienced his strong emotions. What tempestuous emotions seized him after he comprehended the concept denoted by the Russian word for *transubstantiation* only when he discovered its Ukrainian equivalent! Well, what followed? If he had not even associated with that group of Ukrainian friends several years previously, he would still be sitting in this same house, because he would have been invited by the brother of his mother, who taught Russian language and literature, not the Ukrainian trumpet. His thoughts took leaps and bounds and then they vanished; he needed to write them down, but he didn't even pick up his pen and he didn't put a single sheet of paper in the typewriter.

But he thought: if he were to write, then it would only be philosophical essays, and never pitiful literary prose. Who needed another feeble biography? Only principled narratives that scaled the heights of mystery were worthy to be immortalised. In their community there were several writers who published their works in literary journals. On the pages of the *Suchasnist* journal he read with some interest contributions by his acquaintances, recognising in them certain factual aspects of their shared existence. But he found no real inspiration in any of these texts. He pushed the periodical away and reached for the philosophy books, since only they were capable of creating the chaos which, under favourable circumstances, can give rise to a scheme for a dancing star. What makes living in this world worthwhile, actually? In agitation, he got up from his chair, paced around the big house, then went and stood in the doorway, observing the Milky Way and the shooting stars. These flashes of light were supposed to evoke in him a joyful mood. But that did not happen and he went to bed, shelving his unthought-through ideas.

After nights like this he would go for a morning walk in the forest, wandering among the gothic pines, sometimes secretly taking a notebook and pen with him; apparently he worked on his dissertation even in the forest, because there too he met his benefactresses (aka hatchet women) who called out to him, asking how things were, how his work was getting on, and how the dissertation was going. He greeted them in a mechanical way, meanwhile listening to the strange sound up above; he looked up and saw the pines converging at an unattainable height. He felt that if he kept on walking among the pines for a long time he would be bound to emerge at the seashore. But the forest was becoming ever more dense and more gloomy. It was a particularly hot day, so the gloomy forest was enticing. The pines reminded him of music by the two Richards — Wagner and Strauss, and also of the writings of Nietzsche, which were above all musical. If only he could read them in the original! He walked on and now there were no people around and he had the feeling that he was prepared to wander in this forest until the end of his life, when, exhausted, he would fall at the foot of a reverberating pine tree and fall asleep for all eternity.

But suddenly the forest came to an end. Ahead of him there was boundless space with no signs of life whatsoever. No human life. The fragrant grasses whispered, birds screeched, and some creatures he could not see, and did not want to see, made a rustling sound amongst the grass. He wanted to go home, but he did not know the way. Leaving the forest behind him, he walked across the fields, following a path which kept winding around, leading goodness knows where. And now he had even lost sight of the forest; all around him there was nothing but the plain. Snatches from songs about *A Path in the Middle of the Fields* that was *The One and Only Path* came into his head. What idiots composed those songs! These paths lead nowhere! Why hadn't he stayed in the forest? There he could have found some berries at least! There he could have sat down under a pine tree! Instead of walking in the midst of the fields under the scorching sun, following a path that led to the end of the world!

It seemed that if he followed this path back he would return to the forest; at least the sun would not be beating down there. But the peculiar nature of this space is such that if you follow the same road back you do not get back to where you started from.

God, how dreadful! A healthy man at the peak of his strength went for a walk in the forest and got lost! And he can't find his way back home! What a humiliating state of affairs! What stupid forces had dragged him to this Irivka! When he got lost once in New York, he worked it out in the space of ten minutes! Whereas here it could all be over for you! How long had he been walking since the morning? His wristwatch had stopped. He was lost in both space and time. The path wound its way among the grass like a snake, not leading anywhere. Or did it lead to Hades — it was hot enough. Here he was; this was the flip side of making contact with the elements. In the sea, in the mountains, in the forest and on the steppe it was possible to get lost and not find your way out, and instead of elation you experienced terror.

But this is not the steppe zone! In this region you have to search hard if you want to find a boundless space like that! And yet! … Just as he was ready to fall on his back in the grass, stretch out his arms and await his end beneath the scorching sun, he caught sight of two female figures up ahead.

5. All the folklore

Despite the extreme heat, his hunger and the terror that had just overwhelmed him, Eugene recognised one of the girls. It was she who had brought him the amazing apples a few weeks previously and asked to be shown round the house. At the time, he hadn't asked her name. The other girl looked much younger, although they were both of the same height.

The girl recognised him too. But he regained his presence of mind, succeeding in concealing the despair he had just succumbed to. He struck up a conversation with the girls just as if nothing had happened. But he confessed to being lost. Could the little ladies show him how to get back home?

"You townies never know how to follow our footpaths," said the girl he knew, rather arrogantly, while the other one countered her remark, pointing out:

"But townies know lots of other things that we don't. Have you forgotten that you couldn't find the college of medicine in Kyiv?"

"A good job I didn't! I found one nearer to home," retorted the other girl.

"A good job for me too! I met these young ladies in the middle of a field!" he said, using bland expressions he never liked, just to prevent the girls quarrelling.

The girls laughed disarmingly. Since he was bound for Irivka, they were all going the same way, they said. It turned out that the girls were called Olya and Tanya, that they were twin sisters, fraternal, not identical, that Olya was the one who brought him the apples, that she had been studying for two years at the regional college of medicine and had two more years to go, while Tanya had another year at school, only she went to school in Kobivka, not in Irivka, because her parents were teachers at the Irivka school. She wanted to go on to university, in Kyiv of course. The girls had just been to Kobivka to have their fortunes told.

"Well, and? Did they tell you your true fortunes?"

"They told Olya's," replied Tanya.

"What about yours?"

"There isn't anyone for me to have my fortune told about yet!" replied Tanya; at that Olya started whispering to her sister, trying to tell her something without Eugene hearing, so once again he had to steer the conversation in such a way as to prevent the sisters arguing.

"Forgive me, girls. As you correctly pointed out, I am a townie, so there are lots of things around here I am unfamiliar with, but as far as I am aware fortunes are told at night-time, in the moonlight, not in broad daylight."

"But our mother won't let us out at night," replied the girls.

"So you do what your mother tells you?"

The girls laughed for ages, until they set him off as well.

"Do you do as your mother tells you?" they enquired.

"Sometimes."

It occurred to Eugene that he was here in this village — this *Idiotivka*, as he sometimes called Irivka in his mind — precisely because he had done as his mother told him.

"Such a big lad," said Olya, bursting out laughing, and Tanya followed suit. Eugene observed the girls closely. Two fraternal twins should have different colour hair. These two had very similar blonde hair. But Olya looked grown-up; she had all the right attributes, whereas Tanya looked like a child of 12 or 13.

The houses of Irivka came into view ahead of them. He realised that he had skirted round the village at 180 degrees. First through the forest, then across the fields. What sort of warped space is this round here? You keep walking straight ahead all the time, but in the end you find you are not moving in a straight line but following a curve, and a very marked curvature at that.

"Let's all go to ours for dinner," said the girls. "Our mum will be absolutely over the moon."

He was so hungry that it seemed he wouldn't make it home, and on top of that he would have to peel the potatoes and boil them; he didn't think he had any bread, and speck is not much good without bread. So he accepted the invitation, although he realised it would mean getting even more deeply involved in the mundane way of life of Irivka.

The moment he crossed the threshold, following the girls, one of his 'suppliers' rushed towards him, the one who had dreams about a wedding and about black birds above the General's house. At first, the hostess froze at the sight of her daughters arriving in the company of an esteemed guest, clapping her hand to her mouth, but then she began to sing out loud, dancing to the song:

> *Oh, green is now the rye, the rye!*
> *Oh, here an honoured guest have I!*

Eugene, who had by now recovered from the excessive heat and from the shock, felt like escaping despite his hunger, so as to avoid participating in this crazy spectacle. The girls, meanwhile, filled some large enamel bowls with water from an enormous bath standing out in the sun, added handfuls of soap powder and sat down on stools by the porch to wash their feet, cleaning the soles with little scrubbing brushes. They paid no attention to their mother, who broke off without finishing the folk song, shouting:

"Misha! Misha! Do you know who our visitor is? We've been waiting for the girls for ages, telling them off, and now they turn up with a visitor like this! Oh dear me! And all I've got is my fasting borshch!"

They laid the table outdoors. Amongst the bowls of borshch appeared pickled gherkins, little bowls of garlic and onion, glasses of moonshine and, naturally, speck.

"Come on, help yourselves, it's all home-made. You won't get anything like this in town!"

He was by now used to this byword that accompanied all meals in the village.

"So your mother is unwell?" Eugene was asked by the hostess, whose name was Zoya Mykolayivna.

"Oh no, why do you ask?"

"Well, she didn't come to the General's funeral because she was sick."

Eugene recalled the falsehood that his mother had permitted him. He had already forgotten about this, but the women of Irivka remembered it very well, and so he was obliged to extricate himself from the situation.

"Yes, it's chronic; she's ill the whole time. My father and I have got used to it."

"She doesn't work then?"

"She works very hard, actually. She has great difficulty walking, but she still goes to work."

"What sort of work does she do?"

"She's a teacher of Russian literature."

Zoya Mykolayivna began clapping her hands, jumping for joy.

"So we're colleagues then! Both teachers of Russian, and that means foreign literature now! What a shame she was taken ill! She and I would have had a lot to talk about.

"Perhaps she would have enjoyed speaking Russian with you!" said Zoya Mykolayivna's husband, who had been silent until then. He had a rather strange accent, pronouncing the vowel 'a' where in Ukrainian there would have been an unstressed 'o'.

"You should have kept quiet, Mykhailo Tykhonovych," shouted the hostess at her husband, and Eugene recalled Volodya's words about the women of this village and how they hen-pecked their husbands. Was this the Tykhonovych that

Volodya would treat even though he was a Muscovite? Zoya Mykolayivna poured second helpings of borshch for the men, and she started telling Eugene if not her entire life story then at least its main stages.

She was born nearby, in Kobivka. But do you know what *kobi* means? *Kobi* means sorcerers. She went to school there too. When she left school she went to the regional teacher training institute. She met Tykhonovych at the railway station. He was so handsome, just out of the army! He wondered whether he should go back to his home in the Pskov region or stay here.

"Should have gone back!" said Tykhonovych.

"Aha! Have you forgotten the fact that your three brothers had become drunkards in that Erokhivka of yours, and that one of them had died?"

"Erokhino, you Ukie! You can't even pronounce the name of the place correctly!"

"Oh shut up, Tykhonovych, you bloody russki! Stop interrupting me!" said Zoya Mykolayivna, cutting her husband short and turning to her guest again. "You see, this lad, this Mikhail that's sitting here opposite you, he was handsome when he came out of the army, and he was my heart-throb then, in my young days, so I persuaded him to become a student along with me in the Russian department at the University. He hadn't intended to become a university student at all; he was thinking of being just an ordinary worker. But we entered the university together; we both failed to make the grade for Russian, but we both got in to take Ukrainian, where the competition wasn't so stiff."

"But how did Mykhailo Tykhonovych manage to pass a test in Ukrainian if he had never studied it?" enquired Eugene, crunching on a pickled gherkin.

"Well, he'd just come out of the army, you see! Men like him were not left out on the street in those days; if they wanted to study they would get in somewhere. Besides, friendship of peoples was the watchword then."

Zoya did well at the education faculty, so she was able to transfer to the Russian department later, while Tykhonovych went on to complete his studies in Ukrainian. And then the girls were born. Two of them at once! Tykhonovych wanted to call them Marusya and Oksana. But Zoya Mykolayivna said: "Over my dead body! They will be called, as in Pushkin, Tatiana and Olga!"

"That's the six hundred and twenty eighth time they've said that," said Olya with a heavy sigh.

"It might be the six hundred and twenty ninth, so what? I love Pushkin above all else. Whenever I start reading Onegin, I can't put it down:

> *Tatiana's walks get longer still,*
> *A hillock here, and there a brook*
> *That slow her down against her will,*
> *She's led into a shady nook!"*

You couldn't tell if it was supposed to be Russian or Ukrainian as Zoya Mykolayivna recited her own version of these lines from the novel in verse. My dear mother should be here, thought Eugene. She is convinced that there is nobody in Ukraine who doesn't know the Russian language. What a glorious refutation of his mother's notion this teacher of Russian language in Irivka is! So much effort, and yet she can't string two words together in Russian!

"Oh you just shut up, Tykhonovych!" Zoya Mykolayivna descended from her exalted poetry to address her husband: "Tanya and Olya are the most beautiful girls' names in the world!"

"But there are always nine Tanyas and Olyas in every class!"

"What about the Oksanas and Marusyas?"

"Fewer, fewer! This isn't my first year at the school!"

"I would like to be Maria," said Olya.

"You would be Oksana!" replied Tanya.

"No, you would be Oksana," said Olya, getting angry. The

girls started to quarrel; what a strange thing to be arguing about! Evidently, the topic of their names was a source of endless quarrels in their family.

"Quiet, girls, quiet!" shouted Zoya Mykolayivna to her daughters. "Quiet! Quiet!"

After repeating "Quiet!" several times, she began to sing this word rather than saying it, then she drew it out:

"Quiet by-y the brook! Da-ark night-ti-ime!"

"The charmed forest is asleep!" Tykhonovych took up the refrain, and as he sang he articulated the Ukrainian words much better than when he spoke. The duet by Zoya Mykolayivna and Mykhailo Tykhonovych sounded wonderful. Eugene even found it enjoyable to listen to them, as had been the case previously too, when the villagers of Irivka had begun to sing spontaneously. Sometimes it is better to sing than to speak.

The relationship between Mykhailo Tykhonovych and Zoya Mykolayivna by no means represented the relations between Russia and Ukraine, in a historical, political or cultural sense. But they bore witness to something. As would become clear, Tykhonovych was not simply a teacher of Ukrainian language and literature at the Irivka secondary school, but he was also the head of the official regional association of teachers of Ukrainian, because he was the only male teacher in these parts. Lada should come here. Only she, after her studies at leading European universities, would be able to distinguish the patriarchal discourse of authority from the post-colonial syndrome.

"Do you know what they call me in Irivka, Eugene?" asked Zoya Mykolayivna, suddenly cutting short her singing. "You'll never guess. The singing mother-in-law!"

"You aren't a mother-in-law yet, though!"

"But I have two daughters!"

"Mum, give it a rest! We're fed up of hearing this!" called out the girls.

"Yes, you should stop banging on about it! You'll be a granny before you are a mother-in-law," said Tykhonovych.

"You as well, Dad, shut your mouth! Hold your gob, as they say here in Ukraine! Times are quite different now," said Olya, continuing some old family debate.

Tykhonovych re-filled the glasses.

"I won't pour any for you," he yelled at his daughters, in feigned outrage.

"Look, we don't need your moonshine anyway," burst out Olga, who was fond of picking a quarrel with everybody in turn.

After Eugene had dined at the Singing Mother-in-Law's house, the women started visiting him less frequently, but he had plenty of produce in any case. On the other hand, Tanya and Olya began to visit. The girls came together and their company was more congenial than the visits of the Vegetable Woman and Her who brings the milk. Generally speaking, things got better. Obviously, these women had given up; the Singing Mother-in-Law had won out, they said. Christ! — he thought — they're matching me with one of these brainless girls! Just what I need after Lada, the intellectual! But which of them should I choose? Olya, although she had an unpleasant disposition, was ten times sexier. But Tanya was quite juvenile.

Time was flying by; it was already the middle of August. How quickly time passed, especially in summer! A rainy period set in. The General's house shuddered under the downpour, and that was a good thing, because it brought on strange sensations. He was sitting there with no bread, but he had potatoes and a tub of crunchy gherkins which Tykhonovych had brought him on his cart. There was speck and onions. There were the preserves in the cellar; recently he had opened a jar of last year's tomatoes, because, as he had been told repeatedly, there would be no tomatoes in Irivka this summer. He also had several bars of chocolate and his uncle's cognac. Let the rain continue, as long as he had supplies.

In the evenings the rain pelted down especially meaningfully, carrying messages which he thought he could begin to decode if he shut all everyday matters out of his head. Suddenly, he began to re-live a forgotten, quite unremarkable time in his life, when as a little eight or nine year old lad he had been taken by his father and mother to a holiday hotel in the Kyiv region, where it had started to rain just like now.

"We've come for a holiday!" said his mother, laughing. "To go down to the river and bask in the sunshine!"

They didn't go back home; they ran to the dining room through the rain and spent the rest of the time in their room, listening to the sound made by the rain. His mother read some book and hardly talked to him, for which he felt belatedly grateful to her now as he recalled those days, because it was then that he first began thinking about the meaning of existence. Thinking pleasurably, almost going into a trance as he contemplated why it was pouring with rain and why he was so unexpectedly enjoying the view from their room of the wet wild vines entwining the shabby veranda of the adjoining hotel building. Now he had a view of the door to the store-room, entwined with wild vines. Only now did he notice the peculiar architecture of this edifice, which he had been looking out onto from the window for ages. What a strange gable end that was, surmounting the metal-framed doorway to the premises where he kept the potatoes!

In the evening, in spite of the incessant rain, Volodya turned up. At first, Eugene was not pleased to see his visitor, because he was just getting engrossed in *Ecce homo*. But he could not send the young doctor back home in the rain. He knew Volodya lived with his sick mother in a small house at the opposite end of the village, near the family of the Singing Mother-in-Law. So he invited him into the living room and, as usual, he took out a bottle of cognac and some chocolate. Why has he come to see me when it's raining so hard? Was he missing our evening discussions?

After the first glass, Eugene felt at ease with Volodya again. The young doctor decided the time had come to reveal to the General's heir the whole truth about the house he was living in. More precisely, to acquaint him with the versions of it which were current in Irivka. According to one of the versions, this house brought misfortune, according to another it initiated paranormal phenomena, which did not portend happiness either.

To begin with, apparently nobody knew who built this house or when, and the documentation had not survived. But this was not surprising, since on this very geographical eminence was the site of the sorcerers' sabbath where the Kobi assembled. In this very place stood their tent, beneath which they boiled their herbs in a large cauldron. The Iri were afraid of the Kobi, although the latter had never done the former any harm. They did not associate with one another, but one day a girl from the Iri fell in love with a Kobi boy. Then the Iri cunningly deceived the Kobi and chased them away. Or, as they also tell, while the wedding of the Iri girl with the Kobi boy was taking place, the Iri took the magic Kobi cauldron and hauled it off to the place where Kobivka is now. It is in a depression, a damp place where it's difficult to build…

"So the Kobi are sorcerers. But who are the Iri?"

"The Iri are the inhabitants of Iria, in other words paradise, as they used to call it."

"So Irivka is a place of paradise then?"

"Yes, something like that. But when the Iri chased the Kobi away there was no longer a paradise in Iria. It became Irivka, not Iria any longer."

"What an original version of the banishment from paradise! Tell me more, Volodya. Why didn't you speak of this before?"

"Well, I was afraid I would scare you."

"But I would like to know. Tell me more!"

"They say the Iri castrated this Kobi, who… well, you know."

"But why?"

"So he would keep away from what wasn't his."

"You mean for ideological reasons?"

"It is also said that all the Kobi were castrated…"

"But that would have been difficult in practice!"

"Then how do you explain the fact that all the boys in Irivka keep wetting their pants until they go to school? This is not the case in Kobivka. That's why the children at Irivka nursery school are all girls!"

After the Kobi were driven out, according to folk tradition, Iria ceased to exist. The crops failed and pestilence struck the cattle and the Iri themselves. Then the Iri started calling the Kobi back again. They replied that it was no longer in their power to restore paradise to Iria, and that an outsider would have to come and settle on the site of the Kobi sorcerers' sabbath and fall in love with an Iri girl or a Kobi girl. Then he would acquire the power of the former Kobi and paradise would return to Irivka.

Eugene had the feeling that the naïve *folklore* was not the main reason for Volodya's visit when it was raining so hard. And he was right. That evening Volodya revealed his whole secret to him. Apparently, he had tender feelings for Olya, the nurse-to-be. He was troubled by the fact that the girl was so young, only fifteen, and he had imagined himself marrying someone older. But he had personally arranged for this child to attend the college of medicine, so they could work together. It is a very good thing when the village doctor and the nurse are married. They were not going out together yet, but in December they would be free to do so, when the girls would be sixteen.

Eugene was touched by Volodya's confession and somewhat embarrassed by it, because of course in the village of the *honest uncle, beyond reproof* the classic story of Russian literature was continuing to unfold. Was such a set-up a harbinger of doom? The outsider Eugene in their village, the engagement of Olga, the dispute between Vladimir and Eugene, the duel… At first, Volodya did not grasp what he was talking about or what he meant by the duel. Eugene had to remind the young doctor at some length of the great cultural narrative which had slipped Volodya's memory. Finally, Volodya understood.

"We were all given such ordinary names! When I was a medical student, there were eight Volodyas in our year and seven, no… Volodya began counting on his fingers … nine Olgas! And the lecturer in political economy was Oleksandr Sergiyovych, well, so what? Did that make him a Pushkin?"

"But Zoya Mykolayivna told us she purposely named the girls in honour of Pushkin's Tatiana and Olga."

"Yes, she tells everybody that! Four times a day!"

"The Singing Mother-in-Law…"

"What's to be done about that now? We'll have to get a place built. The one I live in with my mother is too small…"

The rain stopped and on the first sunny day Tanya came on her own, without Olya.

"I wonder if I could read one of the books you have here…"

"The kinds of books I have wouldn't interest you, Tanya."

"Oh, why not?"

"Well, just have a look for yourself," he said, showing the girl to his desk in the study in the north wing. "Choose something. What would you like?"

Tanya looked at the two-volume sets of Nietzsche and Francis Bacon and at Kundera's *Immortality*. Eugene knew that there existed child prodigies in the town who read something similar while they were still of school age. He was somewhat envious of them, because when he was a schoolboy he read and understood *The Red and the Black* and *The Catcher in the Rye* in the original; he read and re-read *The Master and Margarita* and much else besides, but when he was at school Nietzsche was just not around! He wondered whether he would have coped with him then. Eugene knew, too, that sometimes there were clever boys and girls from the country at university in Kyiv, who also successfully absorbed all that. But this was not such a case. Tanya spent a long time looking at the books, then she said:

"I've brought you something to read too."

"She took out of her shoulder bag a *Harlequin Pocket Book* from the *Great Passions* or *Enchanted Love* series, or something of the sort, and offered it to him. Oh dear! *She was fond of novels at an early age.* But of course in the classical Russian story they were novels by *Richardson* and *Rousseau*! Goodness knows who that Richardson was, but well, Rousseau is Rousseau. It seems the classical young lady read the great representative of the Enlightenment only for the narrative, but here it was some Nora Roberts or Bertrice Small. Lada reviewed this literature for girls with reading difficulties, pointing out that reading matter such as this not only reinforced their backwardness but encouraged them to accept traditional gender roles.

"Take it, go on!" insisted Tanya.

"I've read this, Tanya," he said, lying uneasily.

Tanya then immediately wanted to discuss the book, which had made a big impression on her, with her older friend.

"Susan is brilliant, isn't she?"

"Absolutely brilliant," agreed Eugene. "To do something like that!"

"What was it she did?" asked Tanya craftily.

"What do you mean? She made Robert marry her!"

"Oh no, it wasn't like that at all! You haven't read this book! Here, read it, go on! You'll find it very worthwhile!"

This upset Eugene. The importunate behaviour of the naïve Tanya mirrored the manners of the older Irivka women, constantly doing their utmost to get him to drink their disgusting milk, so he replied a little sharply:

"My dear Tanya, I'm very busy! I'm writing a dissertation. I haven't got time for girlie books!"

"Oh, sorry, Mr Samarsky... I thought you would be interested to read how Susan graduated from the university and how only then George fell in love with her..."

Oh, I see! It isn't so simple! Even on the pages of harlequinesque novels new ideas turn up now! Tanya pulled such a sad face that he immediately sought to rectify the situation.

"Thank you, Tanya. Listen to me! Why do you address me formally? I'm like a school-teacher to you, aren't I? But we're friends, surely?"

Tanya's child-like face remained extremely sad, and he simply couldn't stand it. A radical solution was needed. He recalled what Volodya had recently told him about the Kobi and the Iri.

"Tanya, you said you and Olya went to Kobivka to have your fortunes told."

"Yes," said Tanya, a little more cheerfully. "Do you need yours telling too?"

"You see, Tanya, my wife and I are separated; she didn't want to live with me. She had a son."

"But isn't he yours, Mr Samarsky?" Goodness — this child knows about him too.

"But nobody knows that for certain, do they! Tanya, I thought we agreed to be on informal terms."

"Demyanivna can tell your fortune, Zhenia. If she agrees to see us, that is. She doesn't take any payment."

Eugene recalled the numerous posters in Kyiv during those years, aggressively summoning the people of Kyiv and visitors to the city to séances with fortune-tellers or folk healers who hired large concert halls to peddle their nonsense. He also recalled that a year or two ago on the Khreshchatik he had met an old acquaintance from his pre-Ukrainian life; she proudly explained that she was working as a fortune-teller and making good money, because people were stupid. Why not make money out of people's stupidity? Isn't Demyanivna a similar case? Well, why not take a walk over to neighbouring Kobivka, where he had never been yet? They say that genuine fortune-tellers and healers never take payment. However, *folklore* incorporates fundamental mythological structures. You just needed the skill to recognise them in the chaotic stories told by uneducated villagers. Many different layers of this mythology occur in the story of the Iri and the Kobi.

"Won't you give me any of your books to read?" asked Tanya, interrupting his thoughts.

"Well, perhaps I should give you one of my uncle's books?" Eugene took Tanya to his uncle's wing, showed her the bookcase in the General's study, and took Hemingway's *Farewell to Arms* from its shelf. On his own desk remained the book from the harlequinesque series by an author whose name he had forgotten, though the title of her book stuck in his memory for a long time: *A Mid-Atlantic Encounter*.

Summer was drawing to a close. Tanya did not visit him. The Feast of the Transfiguration, Ukrainian Independence Day and the Feast of the Assumption came and went, and Tanya still hadn't appeared, and the realisation caught up with Eugene that he hadn't gone home for his warm autumn things because he was waiting for Tanya so as not to miss the opportunity to go to Kobivka to see Demyanivna the fortune-teller. He didn't exactly spend days on end waiting for Tanya to turn up, but from time to time he did think of the child with a warm smile.

On the other hand, Olya called round twice. She brought him apples, different ones now, big red ones which were not as unusual to the taste as those she brought in July. Olya exclaimed:

"It's rather untidy here! Come on, quick! Get the broom and sweep up the kitchen!"

"Yes, colonel!" He laughed, touching his temple with his right hand, imitating a military salute, but he didn't take the broom; he didn't even get up from the table, so Olya wouldn't see his involuntary male interest in her. It was only Volodya who, being in love, thought of her as though she was still a child.

"Where did you get Tanya's book from? Does she come to see you often?"

"She was here one day. We exchange books. Perhaps I could give you something to read too?"

"Oh, there's no need, really! I wouldn't advise you to read a lot either. It's better to learn how to give injections."

Tanya turned up on the last day of summer. She had brought back his *A Farewell to Arms*. She liked it a lot. She said she cried when Catherine was dying. Eugene wanted to ask her whether, since she liked this novel by Hemingway so much, which was commendable, she didn't feel there was a difference between it and *A Mid-Atlantic Encounter*. But was it worth the effort to educate the intellectually hopeless Tanya? The girl added that she had also read *The Old Man and the Sea*. In English! They had read an adaptation during lessons at school.

They went to Kobivka. Tanya said it was best to go through the forest and then across the fields, because if they went through the village the eyes of the entire population would be on them. So they took the path through the pine trees. On the way, Tanya told him a lot of interesting things. She said that her darling sister Olya had had her eye on Doctor Volodya for a long time now, ever since he had returned from medical school, in fact. She came to see him at the hospital and said she was going to study at the college of medicine and afterwards she would be working with him, because their medical assistant Nina Pavlivna was due to retire. Their mother had always taught them that if you want a husband you have to pick a lad and treat him from the outset as if he was your husband, shouting at him, even if he does everything as he is supposed to, but looking after him as well, asking if he is hungry, say, or whether he needs anything. That's what Olya did with Volodya, and it seems to have worked. But when you turned up in the village, Eugene Whatsyourname, Olya decided to switch to you, but Volodya's hooked now, which is why that time…"

"Volodya's much better than me! Tell that to Olya!"

"But you've got the General's house, haven't you!" said Tanya, outspokenly.

"Tell your sister I intend to sell the house. Just as soon as I am in a position to deal with it."

They came out of the forest and took the path across the fields. As it turned out, there were several paths in those fields; they were hidden in the grass and they criss-crossed one another. If you take the wrong one, you end up somewhere else, as had already happened to him before.

"How do you know which path to take, Tanya?"

"Well, how do you know which street to take in the town?"

As they were walking along the path across the fields, Tanya told him that, according to Demyanivna, her fate was not yet determined. There were not yet any signs to be read. It was unusual in a girl of her age; in most cases everything was already quite clear. At any rate that is what the fortune-teller said the day we met in the middle of this field, remember? Besides that, as her sister Olya said, Demyanivna told her that day that she and Volodya would be together. But she had said it with a little sadness somehow; well, perhaps it was Olya who said it with a little sadness.

They reached Kobivka and Eugene felt he had been misled. Just as Irivka did not give the impression of being a paradise on earth, Kobivka did not appear to be the habitat of numerous sorcerers either. An inconspicuous village street with fencing, dark foliage and little brick-built houses with painted wooden verandas. One of these dwellings was where Demyanivna lived. Only hers was not directly on the street, but set back from it. Between two stretches of land there was a narrow path where Tanya turned off; he followed in her footsteps.

In the yard a little dog started whining. Tanya waited until the woman, by no means an old granny, came out onto the veranda and ordered the dog to be quiet. Then she invited them indoors.

The room they entered from the veranda was rather small, with practically no furniture except for a table without any tablecloth, and two benches. The walls were starkly whitewashed, with no pictures or rugs. Only dried sprigs with red berries, probably viburnum, hung here and there on the walls. Smooth, broad floorboards, no curtains on the windows. Eugene felt an unexpected draught in the room and he became apprehensive. He felt cold, although he was warmly dressed. It was as though some large, alien space had entered the room. It was the second time that he had been impressed by an interior. The first time was in his childhood, when his mother had taken him to visit her friend Iryna Romanivna, who had a large room in a communal flat on Lviv Square. Since then, neither the large houses on

Pushkin Street nor the mansions of his American colleagues had aroused in him such an almost heart-stopping delight as he suddenly felt in this rustic room.

Demyanivna sat by the table and invited them to sit down opposite her. She was a handsome woman, though she was not young, and slim, which was unusual in country women, who for the most part became shapeless with age. The only concession to tradition was the head-scarf she wore in the style of the Ukrainian *ochipok*,[*] completely concealing her hair. But there were no special effects, no alarming, menacing glances, no theatrical gestures. They talked for a while, like ordinary acquaintances. There were no cups or glasses or books on the table. They talked in a relaxed manner, mentioning that summer was over and school would start the next day. Your last year, Tanya. And how are you getting on here, Eugene, er — I don't know your surname. Have you completed the formalities regarding the inheritance of the house? Do you like living there? Then Demyanivna suddenly said:

"Tanya, go and see why Irchyk is barking like that."

Actually, the little dog was silent. But Tanya obediently went out, and Demyanivna stood up; Eugene, as though seized by some spasm, leaped up as well. A hot flush suddenly came over him, although till then he had felt uncomfortably cold.

"You can't arrange everything as if it was pre-ordained, Zhenia. You'll be uneasy abroad. You won't be able to find your old self again."

As she spoke these three sentences, she addressed Eugene by the short form of his Christian name, although both before and afterwards she addressed him more formally. He seemed to be hypnotised and he didn't ask for any explanation, but followed her towards the door as though driven by some force. As he

---

[*] *Ochipok*. Traditional Ukrainian headwear of married women. It used to be considered proper for the hair of a married woman to be completely concealed.

passed through the veranda forming a hallway, he caught sight of himself in a dusty mirror covered with cobwebs, not as he was then, but much older, with a grey moustache, his hair noticeably thinning. This apparition lasted a few seconds, but the terrifying sensation persisted for a long time afterwards. Why hadn't he stopped in front of this mirror? Then he would have realised that it was all a figment of his imagination. Of course it was an optical illusion — something that everyone experiences from time to time.

Tanya was waiting for them outside. He set off along the path, reached the gate and turned round. During the few moments when Tanya paused by Demyanivna's house, the latter must have said a few meaningful words to her.

"Good luck to you," said Demyanivna, closing the gate after them. "I hope everything turns out for the best. Both for you and for Tanya."

They walked back in silence. No sooner had they emerged from the forest, approaching Irivka, than Tanya, without saying goodbye, ran off home down the street, while Eugene made his way to the General's house.

Back at home, he went over in his mind what Demyanivna had said, and then for some reason he noted it down: You can't arrange everything as if it was pre-ordained. You'll be uneasy abroad. You will be a changed person and you'll lose touch with your homeland. You won't be able to find your old self again.

6. A boring, joyless time

He spent all autumn in Irivka. He bought firewood, because nobody intended to give him any, as it turned out. People who buy it in the village because they don't grow their own don't share it with anyone. The firewood reduced his savings considerably, as it cost ten million.

But they taught him how to stoke up the stove at no cost. He was adept at placing a log on a stand and chopping it with a small axe. In the autumn the women hardly ever visited him, but one day they brought him two bags of potatoes on the cart. The autumn rainy season began. He didn't leave the house. He didn't need to go anywhere. Sometimes it was easy for him to think and read, and at other times it was boring and unpleasant. A life without responsibilities is also a burden not everyone is able to cope with. The sooner he was abroad, where he would be uneasy, the better. He would surely be given a scholarship in America. Well, how else would he be able to go abroad?

Once the weather began to improve, he managed to get to Kyiv for a day. He found out that no notification had come from America and that nobody had telephoned or offered any work either. He exchanged some more dollars and received hundreds of thousands of coupons, bought some coffee and went back to Irivka.

The way across the fields after getting off the train, when the wind is so strong, is quite an ordeal for a town dweller. So when Tykhonovych, on his way from the district centre where he had been attending a meeting of the professional association of Ukrainian language teachers, waved to him and offered a lift, Eugene immediately accepted.

But Tykhonovych took him to his own house, not to the General's.

"You are in need of a meal after your journey and Zoya Mykolayivna has got it all ready. Home-made cockerel borshch."

Yes, the phonetics of a foreign language is the most difficult thing to master, he supposed, as he listened to Tykhonovych's Russian accent. That applies to all languages. On the train recently he had heard so many people trying to speak Russian but sounding Ukrainian. Here the opposite was the case.

The hosts sat at the table with Eugene and Tanya. Olya was in town; she was in her second year at college. Sometimes she came home when she had a day off, sometimes she didn't. Tanya is silent, but she is listening attentively. This was the first time he had seen her since the visit to Demyanivna's. Zoya Mykolayivna is complaining again that they have issued new directives on the teaching of foreign literature.

"Eugene, you've just been home. Tell me, how is your mother?" This time, Eugene was prepared, so he could give a suitable reply:

"She is unwell, but she is working."

"She ought to have come to the village for the summer. We had such a good summer. There would have been room for everybody in the General's house."

"She's allergic to the village. The country air affects her asthma."

"She's asthmatic, is she? Dear me, how dreadful! Tell me, Eugene, what is your mother's view of the cut-backs in the Russian literature course?"

Eugene couldn't care less what his mother's attitude to all this was. Oh dear, they've dragged me into this primitive household again, and they're involving me in these pointless discussions. Home-made cockerel borshch is fine, of course, after a journey, but those accompanying discussions …

"As a patriot in independent Ukraine, my mother takes a positive view of all this," replied Eugene, thinking that if he had to lie then he would do it in style. "It is too much effort for her to re-train to teach Ukrainian now, but she welcomes foreign literature in the secondary school."

"How can Eugene Onegin not be included?" asked Zoya Mykolayivna in alarm.

"How can Goethe not be included? And Hemingway?" exclaimed Eugene. "And Homer?"

"But that was always for reading after school! I noticed a long time ago that children prefer reading foreign literature. But if you don't introduce Russian literature in class they don't read it."

"Why do we need that sick literature? Russian literature is pre-coital!"

"What?!" The teacher was flabbergasted; she didn't understand this word.

"Well, how can I put it — literature which, unlike any other literature in the world, is opposed to family values."

"What do you mean? Russian literature is one of the greatest world literatures! It is for love!"

"For love, but without intimate relationships! Without coitus, to put it plainly!"

"Coitus shouldn't come into it! You have to get married first!"

"You may be right. But when they are married, is it in order then?"

Zoya Mykolayivna and Mykhailo Tykhonovych chuckled with satisfaction.

"But when it's a case of true love, then there are circumstances when it's possible outside marriage."

"Well, if it really is true love," the family of teachers conceded.

"But Russian literature tells you it isn't possible then either! Because it ends badly! My grandma, my mother's mother, who left high school back in tsarist days, was actually the mother of our General!"

"Oh, Zhenia! The mother of our General, God rest his soul,

went to high school? I always told you he was an exceptional man, Misha! You are exceptional too, Zhenia!"

"I'm unexceptional! But that isn't what I'm talking about, that's too literal. I meant something else. Grandma was always reciting this society poem, ad nauseam: *Only the morning of love is fine, fine are only the first timid encounters!* This also meant that afterwards, when romantic affairs went further, they would turn out badly. Russians are hopeless at love-making! Whatever they do, it's a case of Dostoevskyanism! For this reason *fine are only the first timid encounters.*"

"But what books they are capable of writing!" Zoya Mykolayivna said in defence of the Russians.

"But what is in those books? Only platonic love, with all its agonies! Anna Karenina, when she met Vronsky, merely 'besmirched' her reputation! After they made love for the first time, she told him to 'get out!' Whereas our Ukrainians Mavka and Lukash made love, and everything went well for them! Although they weren't married!"

"You can't tell schoolchildren things like that, though." exclaimed Zoya Mykolayivna.

"But it's all right to pull a girl's knickers off under the desk in class," muttered Mykhailo Tykhonovych.

The dreary autumn was becoming colder and yet more dreary. The days were so short that all you could do was sleep. Nobody visited him now; nobody was stopping him reading great books or improving his German, or writing something of his own. But he lacked inspiration, although everything was peaceful in the house. There was only the creaking of the floorboards in the neighbouring wing, slowly settling back into place an hour after they had been walked on. Or perhaps it was being walked on by the mutilated Kobi who had for some unknown reason been castrated by the stupid Iri in the absurd act of cruelty which they are atoning for to this day?

So when the front door creaked, he thought it was one of them. Footfall in the hallway, in the kitchen. No, there was somebody there. He went to the kitchen and switched on the light. It's Tanya. "Good grief, Tanya, come in. Has something happened? What brings you here all of a sudden at this hour?"

"I wanted to ask you something. The newspaper I brought you. Have you read it?"

Sure enough, a few days previously, on her way from school, Tanya had brought him a newspaper containing — just imagine! — an article on Nietzsche.

"Have a look! It's about your philosopher! Read it — you'll find it interesting!"

A banal little piece, just several hundred words. The editor-in-chief had decided to raise the intellectual level of his wretched publication about seeds and Colorado beetles by including an article on Friedrich Nietzsche. Apparently, the great German philosopher was not an acolyte of Hitler, as they referred to him in the USSR, but quite the opposite. And now Tanya had decided to call round to discuss this article with him. Perhaps to borrow something by the philosopher with the moustache; he had a Ukrainian-style moustache… "Like yours, actually."

"Oh no, Tanya, mine isn't like that."

For some reason Tanya wore a bright lipstick, heavy mascara round her eyes and false eyelashes that were not very well applied. She had never come round after dark before. She had called in several times for lunch after the morning lessons. He had treated her to his fried potatoes. Tanya liked that. He said her parents had treated him to a meal, and now he was treating her. Once he even made her a Turkish coffee. That was on her last visit, when she brought that newspaper.

And now here she was, visiting him at nightfall. It was late autumn and the village was all in darkness quite early. There are no street-lamps lighting up Irivka. Everyone is asleep or watching television. But at his house there is this girl. She had come to tell him that she did not need his General's house and she did not need to get married like Olya. But she wanted to "be his friend". Nobody would find out about this visit to his house.

In winter, when it is dark outside, they miss out on important items of news in the village. Tanya started fitfully sobbing and he gave her a drink of juice from a carton, because the tap water in Irivka is not drinkable. She says: "Believe it or not, here everybody watches *Santa Barbara*; even the school teachers discuss Eden and Cruz with the pupils during their lessons." He takes Tanya into the sitting room, sits her down on the sofa and tells her she will soon be leaving school and she will be going away from this village to study in the town, where everybody watches *Santa Barbara* as well, but at least there is slightly more chance of finding something different. To his misfortune, he takes Tanya by the shoulders, gently, as he would a child. But Tanya takes this as a signal and embraces him round the neck.

He had been on his own for almost a year and he had long since recovered from the exhaustion of the preceding tempestuous years; his masculinity was demanding new transports of passion. It crossed his mind that if Olya offered herself to him he wouldn't be able to resist, but as she approached her sixteenth birthday Tanya looked as if she was thirteen; could he treat a child like that? He was no paedophile; he liked mature heifers. But he had to comfort the child somehow:

"Tanya, my dear, you have everything ahead of you; remember what wise old Demyanivna told you?"

"When we went to see her together that time, she said something different!"

"What was it she said? She told me I would go abroad and nobody knew when I would return! You will meet a good lad before long! I'm just an old goat to you."

"I don't want to get married and I don't want your house. But why don't you want just to be with me anyway? Am I of no interest to you at all?" Tanya still had her arms around his shoulders, clutching convulsively at his shirt. Which soap had she seen that in?

"Tanya, do you want me to undo my trousers right now and get it all out?"

"Why are you saying such horrible things," sobbed Tanya, astonished.

"Well, do you want me to *do* them then?"

"It's love I want. Then it isn't horrible. And I don't have to get married."

"It all comes to the same thing in the end, believe me… Tanya, what we are talking about isn't right. Let me take you home!"

"You don't have to go with me. There isn't anything to be frightened of here in Irivka. I came to see you in good faith. I didn't want anything from you. But you didn't believe me. You thought I wanted to make you marry me, but I just wanted us to be friends." With those last words, she wasn't speaking, she was crying. Then she ran away, gripping in her hands the false eyelashes which had suddenly fallen off onto her cheeks. He stood for a long time in the cold out on the doorstep, staring at the impenetrable November darkness into which Tanya had disappeared.

For several days he was unable to get this episode out of his head. How was he supposed to behave, so as not to offend her? Of course, he could have made a woman of her, without making a mother of her too. She wasn't repulsive to him by any means, but as he was well versed in such matters he knew from the outset what it would have led to, above all for her. This young girl wanted to be loved and she imagined that if I had started to remove her jumper she would have felt something extraordinary. Whatever you did then would be wrong, it would all be so traumatic. Lord preserve us from situations like this …

On the day of the winter equinox the final act of this rural drama was played out. The wind is howling and he is sitting in the warmth of his house. It hasn't snowed yet, and there will not be a white New Year. He will see the New Year in here too. Where is that journey abroad that Demyanivna foretold for him? He doesn't even want to go to America. He is fine here. It will be a shame to sell this house. He will miss it. He has found out what it is probably worth. He will not be able to afford to buy a flat in a decent part of Kyiv; there might just be enough for a two-room one on the outskirts. It would be good to have a flat in Kyiv and this house as well. But that will probably be impossible. He is already starting to miss Kyiv, and that is a good thing. It means he will soon be saying goodbye to this peaceful spot; a new phase of normal existence will begin. In Kyiv, he will definitely miss this house, though, with its spacious rooms and the stove which he has become so expert at heating the place with.

Recently, he had begun doing some good thinking again. Once again, unexpected episodes from his childhood and youth started coming back to him, and he made progress with his German. They say Nietzsche is authentic only in the original. He puts on a CD of Mahler's Third Symphony and adjusts the volume. But the great Germans — Richard Wagner, Richard Strauss and Gustav Mahler — don't like their music to be treated as background sound. They like you to listen only to them. So he stops the CD and listens to the silence. It was not without good reason that his uncle wrote about the creaking of the floorboards. But did he know that was the restless Kobi walking about? The ancestors of the present-day residents of Irivka did something to the ancient sorcerers and now they do not know how to placate them. Perhaps poor Tanya came to save her village, so that an outsider would fall in love with her and she could fulfil some mission… How can some sort of paradise return to this Ukrainian village if total collapse reigns throughout the country? Wages and pensions unpaid, prices rising, hyper-inflation and economic collapse, Russian and American mass culture on the television screens, conscientious Ukrainians are emigrating, and the Ukrainian rural population drunkenly sings Russian songs. Lord, what chaotic nonsense fills his head! The worst of it is when you can't free yourself from the words of others in your thoughts. This sort of chaos cannot give birth to a dancing star. Better put Mahler on again and try to shut the thoughts out.

There is a knock at the door. Not Tanya again, surely? I will have to invite her to listen to some music, classical music. She won't cope with Mahler, but I've got Vivaldi. He goes to the door and on the threshold he sees Zoya Mykolayivna and Mykhailo Tykhonovych.

"Zhenia, my dear! We were getting worried that you weren't going to open the door."

"I was working on the seventh chapter of my dissertation."

"The seventh now! Congratulations! You must come round to ours! We're having a big celebration at home. Our girls are sixteen years old today. Olya has come from town. Tanya wants very much to see you too!"

"But I didn't know anything about it. I haven't even got a present!"

"We sent Tanya over on her way from school so she could invite you in good time. But she was embarrassed and didn't come. She's still just our little girl, you see."

It is quite understandable that the girl did not come to invite him to her birthday party after what had taken place between them. But now her demented parents have come, the Singing Mother-in-Law and the Ukrainianised Russian from Pskov, Tykhonovych. They both speak at once, interrupting one another:

"Your friend Volodya is at our house too."

"He wanted to come to invite you himself."

"We're here with the car, Zhenia. Get in, just come as you are."

"No need for presents!"

"You are our best present!"

And here he is at the Marukhins' — that's their surname. The guests greet his arrival with applause and stop eating momentarily. In the house there are a lot of people, a lot of food and a lot of moonshine. There is nowhere to sit down; they all mingle, treading on one another's toes. Volodya squeezes his hand firmly. Tanya, looking pale, smiles despondently. The village Cleopatra, Olya, is wearing a fluffy sweater with a plunging neckline and tight-fitting jeans. Incidentally, Tanya is wearing the same sweater, but over a shirt, so it does not have the same sexy effect. Besides, Tanya does not have her sister's sumptuous breasts.

They pour him a drink. All the women teachers from Irivka secondary school have turned up to this idiotic party. The head teacher, Hanna Petrivna. She who brings the milk, holding a glass of white coconut liqueur; this is how she demonstrates her refinement, dissociating herself from moonshine while suggesting her association with milk. The Fruit and Vegetable Woman, carrying a large cucumber. When they clink glasses in a toast, she clinks with her cucumber. A saucy young woman flaunting her backside, supplying speck to the guests on little plates.

"What snacks do you take with your state vodka in town? Cheese? Salami? Salmon? Here in the village it's always *sallow*, nothing else! *Sallow, sallow, sallow* — she pronounces *salo*, the Ukrainian word for *speck*, with an English accent. They explain to Eugene that this is Angela, the Englishwoman they decided to keep on at Irivka School, despite the abortion.

At this idiotic gathering he stood there dressed just as he had jumped into the car. He had just grabbed his jacket and put on his boots, so his feet were boiling now. But he hadn't brought a coat, because they said they would take him back as well. That's what you get when you don't know how to refuse. That must be why he *can't arrange everything as was ordained*, as wise Demyanivna had told him. The Singing Mother-in-Law calls for silence, as Eugene Onegin is about to propose a toast.

"To the good health of the Larin sisters!" he declares. Everyone claps as if he has uttered some pearl of wisdom. The idiots! This Ukraine of ours puts up with such as these...

His eyes meet Tanya's unhappy gaze. She seems to be thinking the same as he is, except that she certainly lacks the appropriate vocabulary to describe this rave-up and its participants. After all, he can't find the words for it either. There amongst the crowd he spots Olya. She winks at him. Then she motions to him to go outside. He follows. They go out into the garden. The December wind howls, but after the stifling atmosphere indoors he does not feel the cold and actually he feels fine. Olya's eyes, made up like Cleopatra's, are shining in the darkness. Unlike her sister, she knows how to apply make-up. She is not wearing a coat, only the fluffy sweater with the plunging neckline; he wants to feel her there, but Olya doesn't let him; smiling enigmatically, she leads him off somewhere. He reaches for her allurements, but she runs off — what a little tease! If she lures him round the garden like this, he will get into her knickers just as any young lad would do. But Olya stops and, turning her back to him, audaciously drops her tight jeans, presenting him with her bare backside. The light from the lamp-post lit up in honour of the celebrations is reflected on her youthful, healthy skin. On her left buttock there is a butterfly tattoo. Evidently, Olya wanted to show him this stunner to let him know she had been in town for over a year now, so unlike her clever sister she was not a village girl and she was familiar with all kinds of wondrous ways.

But he is not to taste the fruits of paradise! He is knocked to the ground, he is being stifled, and Olya is screaming. Did she pull up her jeans herself? He hadn't even unfastened his own. He struggles to free himself from Volodya's powerful grip, but it isn't easy. The young doctor breathes moonshine in his face and he is gripping his throat with the clear intention of strangling him. But Volodya is not a very good fighter; he is much better at healing wounds. So Eugene manages to break free of Volodya's grasp and get to his feet. When he subsequently recalled these moments, which had changed his life for ever, he recognised that for some reason he had started to self-reflect, which was foolish in that situation. It was then that he recalled the fight between Lada and Halya, when he had been unable to separate them because they wanted to exclude him from their game by every possible means. But here in the rural environment the patriarchal paradigm applies: men fight. Even though the action was taking place in the village of Irivka, where the women dominated the men. It would have been more logical to thrash the little bitch Olya. However, Volodya attacks him, the friend who knew the secret about him and Olya, though hardly anybody in Irivka had found out about it yet. Men's fights also end more seriously than women's squabbles. Volodya wants to knock him down again, but although he fortunately managed to get up once, Eugene knows he might not succeed a second time. So he pushes Volodya away, to stop him attacking him once more. Volodya falls backwards, hitting his head on the barn steps. Volodya is motionless; there is blood around his mouth and neck. Eugene is dumbstruck.

Olya has long since disappeared, but Tanya comes running up to him. She supports Eugene, who is very unsteady on his feet, almost falling on top of the motionless Volodya. Indoors, they are drinking and partying and nobody has noticed the disappearance of the main participants of the celebrations. Tanya and Eugene kneel down and shake Volodya, who does not move. They both instinctively think of summoning Doctor Volodya, who had frequently resuscitated people after celebrations in the village. But of course it is Doctor Volodya himself who is lying here motionless on the cold December ground. Further guests are meanwhile hurrying to the Marukhins, entering the porch, knocking on the door and they are letting them in.

"I think I have to make myself scarce, before your police take me in," he tells Tanya.

"The last train to Kyiv is at ten," says Tanya.

She takes him to the car in which he was brought here, and she sits behind the wheel.

"Can you drive?" Despite the state he was in at the time, he was surprised.

"My dad taught me."

"But you haven't got a driving licence!"

"We'll drive to the station without hitting the main road. Anyway, Uncle Roman is on duty tonight, our Hanna Petrivna's husband."

They didn't have much time, so Tanya drove at speed along

the frozen paths over the black fields. It was a good thing there had been no snow.

"Tanya, I haven't got a penny on me!"

"Nor have I. But they never check the tickets on this train."

"Tanya, my dear, my pet, go straight to the house — here's the key, take it — in the sideboard, in the soup tureen, there's some money. I've just sold my dollars. There's five million there — take it. Take my passport home with you as well, because it contains my address. They'll find it, of course, if they make a search, but perhaps not straight away."

"Don't worry, everything will be all right! You will reach your goal."

By some miracle they reached the station before ten o'clock. There is nobody on the platform — so much the better, fewer witnesses. In the distance the train is hooting and its lights can be seen. It will stop for a moment at the dilapidated platform. He turns to Tanya, taking her by the shoulders.

"Did you want it with Olya?" she asks in a pained voice.

"There was no love there, Tanya. But nothing happened anyway, although it could have. Men are such swine; you've seen it for yourself of course."

"We won't see one another again, Zhenia!"

"We certainly will see one another! Olya will turn into a corpulent auntie; she won't be able to get through the doorway. But you will be beautiful, sensible and slender and we will meet in the middle of the Atlantic!" For some unknown reason he remembered the title of that novel for women which was still there on his desk, alongside the two-volume works of Nietzsche and Bacon.

He kissed Tanya on the cheek, jumped onto the slippery metal steps and reached the rear platform of the train. Then, unsteadily, he moved into the empty carriage and slumped onto a seat which had been stripped of its imitation leather upholstery. All that remained of some seats in the carriage was the metal frame.

He didn't find even a thousand coupons in his jacket pocket, but he took a taxi at the railway station in Kyiv anyway. The driver didn't get it why this guy was wearing only a jacket when people on the street were in sheepskin coats. When they reached the destination, the taxi driver swore, but accompanied him up to the flat. Mother opened the door to him, exclaiming: "Well, thank goodness!"

"Well, thank goodness!" she repeated. "They've already rung you from the embassy about five times! You have to take your passport to the United States embassy tomorrow morning at nine o'clock. You are supposed to fly off to your placement immediately after the New Year holiday. We sent a telegram to the village. It's a good job you came as soon as you received it!"

"Give me a million, I have to settle up with the taxi driver," he said, interrupting his mother.

"Where am I supposed to find this million you want?" she shrieked. At that point he asked the driver to go into the lobby, but he responded aggressively, insisting that he was going to stay put. So Eugene brushed his startled mother aside and went into the sitting room, drove his father off the sofa, moving it to one side. Pushing aside a small chest of drawers, he retrieved his last hidden stash, consisting of a miserable hundred and fifty dollars. He went back to the driver and offered him fifty dollars, with the words:

"Sorry mate! There you go! And if anybody should ask, you didn't drive me here from the station!"

The driver was happier now, and they shook hands.

"Can you just explain to me what actually happened?" asked his mother.

"Your telegram found me at the Larins' ball. If I had run round home I would have missed the last train. That's why I've turned up here without a coat and without any money."

"That's clear," replied his mother. "Only it isn't clear what the Larins are doing in Irivka."

7. What a Russian story!

The rest of the story takes place in America. Except, of course, for that short period before his departure when he lived in a constant state of terror, fearing that they would come for him and call him to account for the murder he had committed. As far as possible, he kept away from the house, and he did not even see in the New Year, his last New Year in Kyiv, at home with his parents, but with a bottle of beer in the metro, at Khreshchatik station, where besides him there were crowds of other restless folk around. The only thing which gave him comfort at that time was the prophecy made by the fortune-teller Demyanivna of Kobivka: "You'll be uneasy abroad!" If only he could go abroad! Better to be abroad than in prison!

But the nerve-racking phase passed. He experienced a final stomach-churning climax during the passport control at Boryspol airport. When the border guard finally handed back his passport at the checkpoint window, he felt not just relief but that other-worldly light-headedness when your own body becomes weightless and you are at risk of floating up to the ceiling. If they had been searching for him with the intention of placing him under arrest they would not have allowed him through passport control. But here he is, en route to Amsterdam, and transferring to the flight to America. He didn't even know for which city or which university in his new homeland he was bound. But the flight numbers shown on his ticket were clearly displayed on the announcement board, so within a few hours he had reached the correct destination. Anyway, this was not his first visit to America. Of course, he had previously been invited to visit big cities on the Atlantic coast, whereas now he had to fly further on, across a whole time-zone. But Eugene Samarsky successfully completed this journey too, involving a number of changes; he was met and driven to his accommodation, where he was able to get some sleep for the first time since leaving the General's house, which remained in a totally different sphere of existence, one into which he had wandered accidentally, and which had to be put out of his mind. He would begin to work on that a little later, once he had adjusted to the American environment.

Half-way into the period of his placement, when he had to consider not returning, he began to respond to the engaging Dounia Gourman, with whom he had become acquainted at one of the numerous university socials. Dounia had appealed to him immediately, not as a potential wife, but as a friend, as the elder sister he had never had, and would have liked to have at that time. They became quite close, and in due course he told Dounia Gourman about the General's house, about Doctor Volodya, about the little tart Olya, about the touchingly simple Tanya, and also about the secondary participants in that drama. Dounia found all Eugene's experiences in the village of Irivka extremely exciting. She exclaimed:

"What a Russian Story! It's straight out of Dostoevsky!"

After all, the way the Russian story developed in a Ukrainian village was more reminiscent of Dostoevsky than of Pushkin: a young, unspoilt girl, intellectually undeveloped however, offers herself to a mature, highly educated man. The man rejects her because she is not sufficiently mature to tempt him. (Although, actually, behaving in a Dostoevskyan manner would mean taking under-age girls, particularly if they are so forward.) Another young person, a sinful one, a corrupt one, offers herself to the same man, and he is tempted. There is no sophisticated duel with the fiancé of the loose girl and the man she enticed, but a drunken brawl. The enticed man accidentally kills the virtuous fiancé. The first girl, despite having suffered the severe shock of sexual rejection, assists the enticed man to escape from justice. There is a distressing, heart-rending scene at the station in the midst of the fields. The train crosses the boundless Russian steppe; on the enticed man's lips will remain for ever the salt from the tears running down the cheeks of the young girl …

Who is to blame?

All the blame could be placed on the enticed man who killed the fiancé. But he was acting in self-defence; it was either him or his attacker. All the blame could be placed on the fiancé who wanted to kill the enticed man, but he was overcome by a fit of passion and unable to control himself. Again, the blame could be placed on the enticed man, not because he defended himself, but because he succumbed to temptation. But he had been without a woman for a long time, so he could not control himself. All the blame could be placed on the loose young woman, but it is not she who is to blame; it is the primitive circumstances of her life. The girl strove as best she could to find another life, different from that offered by a dull Russian village. The blame could be placed on the other girl, who assisted the enticed man to escape from justice. But she was rescuing the man she loved. And what good would it do if he was condemned to several years in prison for an unpremeditated killing? That would not bring the fiancé back to life.

What was to be done?

Because he was involuntarily enticed by two girls and killed the fiancé of one of them, it is not in his interest to return to his home country. Most likely, no proceedings had been initiated, because if they were searching for him his parents, with whom he spoke on the phone from time to time, would have known about it. But the state of fear was ruining his life. In America, on the other hand, he will be able to dismiss this fear. Interpol will not be looking for the killer of a village doctor, even if they do belatedly open the case.

So what was to be done, actually?

It is possible to live in America on an illegal basis. This is possible; lots of people do live like this. In America there is plenty of work specifically for illegal immigrants in the building trade and on the farms — in their state it is common in both. You can also marry an American woman. Then everything generally becomes very straightforward. All right, their university is no Harvard. But there are great opportunities here too.

It was summer, the unbearable American summer. But, strange to say, there is a breeze blowing on this hill in the midst of the prairie. Above the prairie, swallows are circling. This couple, a thirty year old man from Eastern Europe, intelligent, handsome, dark-haired, with a fine moustache, who has certain problems back home — but who hasn't? — and a slightly older American woman, also attractive in her own way, with luxuriant red hair and pleasant, kindly, freckled features. They are sitting not on a blanket but on folding chairs. Eugene felt even less inclined to embrace the mature Dounia than the immature Tanya a year previously. But at that moment he congratulated himself on reaching *the coast*. The Atlantic coast. Although it was a long way to the Atlantic from the prairie.

He was looking for somebody to confide in about his problems, for which Dounia was his choice. As for Dounia, she was openly, naively and genuinely searching for a young Russian man interested in an academic career in the field of Russian Studies, someone she could give a decent opportunity, for which Eugene was her choice.

In the event, he did not become a Russianist, although Dounia kept prodding him to do so in all possible ways: the daughter of a great Russian 20th century composer used to work in the Russian department at their university, you know! In Ukraine there is a musical group with the same name, replied Eugene, but this was of no interest to Dounia. As your Nietzsche said, Eugene, limited knowledge is wisdom. Knowledge of Ukraine did not figure in Dounia's plans.

You can, of course, devote yourself to something marginal, Dounia thought. A true scholar finds both ideas and their manifestation everywhere. The point is not that Ukrainian Studies is an even narrower field than Irish Studies, which is, however, represented at virtually every university. It is also true that Russian Studies is restricted to the sphere of the universities; it is no Hollywood project. The point is that we are not at Harvard. And if this is how it has turned out, why not get involved in Russian Studies? Is your heart not in it? But why not? Dounia felt she had grasped the crux of the problem, believing that his reluctance to immerse himself in the Russian nineteenth-century golden age was the fault of his mother, who over-enthusiastically sought to 'matchmake' her son with Turgenev's girls, to such an extent that he came to hate them all — Liza Kalitina, Elena Stakhova and Natalia Lasunskaya. And the whole of Russian literature became for him a kind of correct young Turgenev girl, troubled about whether to give herself to some revolutionary, not necessarily a Russian one. Or to take the veil.

"But in Russian literature there are so many fallen women! You could study one of them!" exclaimed Dounia Gourman spontaneously; she genuinely believed that a fallen woman was far more interesting than a so-called pure one. At least to a literary scholar!

He did not want to become a Russianist, but he didn't intend to become a Ukrainian scholar either, and Harvard was beside the point here. If *Harvard* is the apotheosis of an earthly academic career, then wherever he was he would be *not at Harvard*. Dounia could not understand him at all, and he was unable to explain it to her; indeed he did not try. She did not show a trace of the tyrannical wealthy wife so frequently found in her beloved Dostoevsky, so thank goodness for that! You can happily live in America. But in America the Nietzschean spirit vanishes. Although Nietzsche Studies is found in many American universities, not just at Harvard. But hadn't he himself searched for opportunities to remain in America? So who was responsible for the weakening of his will to live? Pushkin? During his childhood there used to be an idiotic saying amongst young schoolchildren: "If something isn't right, whose fault is it? Pushkin's?"

Eugene Samarsky took full advantage of those decent opportunities which this university in the midst of the prairie opened up for him, and, more specifically, his marriage to Dounia. He had been working in administration for over ten years now; on the whole this quite appealed to him, because it gave him the opportunity to meet many interesting people, while someone else wrote the reports. He also has a good part-time job; he receives invitations to act as interpreter at congresses and conferences. Here too, without realising it, Dounia was a support to him. He did not want to speak Russian with her, though he was always ready to explain to her certain finer points in Russian books. However, instead of helping to improve Dounia's command of colloquial Russian, he gradually absorbed her colloquial English, hook, line and sinker, including her sibilant Irish accent. He acquired a better command of English than was necessary in order to merely successfully adjust in the United States. And he became an excellent interpreter.

Life settled down. He now enjoyed pretty much the whole range of earthly blessings. Citizenship of a great country, a house, a job, an intelligent wife, a no less intelligent lover, Halya (the one who once beat up Lada), with whom he communicates in Ukrainian. He also has a son, who acknowledges him as his father, and with whom he also communicates in his native language. The only drawback is that he has no spice in his life. But then who has?

He has no opportunity to travel to his native city. Perhaps this is why he is so fond of the imaginary nostalgic walks around Kyiv, as he remembers it. As he wanders round Kyiv in his mind, a kind of altered state comes over him, akin to a guided dream which would suddenly be sharply and painfully wrested from his control.

Now he is roaming round a cold park by the river Dnipro in early spring or late autumn. The wet benches are devoid of any of the citizens of Kyiv, who in summer leave not a single seat free, whenever you go to that park. Now he is making his way from one park to another across a ramshackle bridge and down below, in the distance, there is a street which he has dreaded seeing ever since his mother used to take him for walks to show him Kyiv when he was a little lad. But he stops to look down, keeping his eyes fixed on the distant pavement.

Here is the stage where the symphony orchestra plays in the summer; at least it did in Soviet times. This is where his parents met. His mother had come along to listen to a concert of classical music. His father fortuitously happened to come along, because they were playing a polonaise by Ogiński, a popular melody which he took an immediate liking to. Now a pack of stray dogs with large sad eyes is lying by the broken-down benches. He watches them for a long time, then he shares with them some biscuits he has in his pocket. Then he goes to the observation platform above the precipice and behind him is the Ukrainian Parliament, and the inevitable demonstrators. He goes to the next park above the Dnipro; it reaches as far as a grey building in the style of the Stalin era. Raising his collar against the cold wind, he walks along Grushevsky Street to the Arsenal underground station. Circumventing the station building, he calls in at a milk bar, in another large grey building, where he drinks coffee leaning against a narrow stand-up table. In America the coffee is worse, in Europe it is better, but coffee like this does not exist anywhere else. As he recalls the cannon on its pedestal that can be seen from the window of the milk bar, imagining it in his mind's eye, his tongue and palate recall that black taste.

The milk bar, where he frequently used to drink cheap but good coffee in the bad old days, is not his only association with this large grey building in the Pechersk District. Here too, the party took place where he met them all — all those people who governed his life for several years, Lada as well. It was a long time ago; the flat was sold during the first years when property sales had become possible, and even if they hadn't sold, their group would have disbanded: *some are not here, and others are not with us*. But from the courtyard you can see that balcony and that porch. You have to go past the grocery shop and through the archway, though. There you will be surprised to see not the lush gardens of a high-class Kyiv building, but a single-storey detached house of ancient grey brick, beyond which, surprisingly, you see boundless fields with flowering herbs. At this very spot something sharply and painfully jolts him out of his drowsy state. He wonders why this break in time and space is so painful for him, since other walks round Kyiv also, sooner or later, lead him to the General's house, a hundred kilometres from the capital.

He has not forgotten anything about what happened to him in that house, in that village. Nothing has been suppressed; he remembers it all. Sometimes he tries to repress these memories. At other times he lowers his resistance and remembers the General's house, the village of Irivka, Olya, Tanya and Volodya. Demyanivna's prophecy had come true. The fifteen minutes, at most, that he had spent in that woman's house still came back to him after fifteen years. He is paying rather a high price for his involuntary crime — for fifteen years now he has been unable to travel to Kyiv, where he very much wants to go.

"You shouldn't have any regrets about Kyiv!" says, consolingly, Halya from Chicago, who occasionally goes to Kyiv. "They are destroying the city; they've gone crazy — there's hardly anything left! The historic city centre has gone! All the open spaces where you once took me for walks are crammed with stupid, inane skyscrapers. Our favourite coffee houses and our favourite bookshops are no more. Don't go to this Kyiv! On your salary you can afford to travel to much more pleasant places! Where is your next congress?"

The congresses and conferences are actually held in the

most unexpected corners of planet Earth. In addition to the well-trodden routes, he has visited Madagascar, Iceland and Indonesia. In November there is a congress in the Azores.

"I'm going with you," says Myroslav. Neither this line from Mayakovsky's poem: *You see, life will pass by just as the Azores passed by*, nor this line from the song by a Soviet bard: *In the city of Ponte Delgado a young girl looks through the window* means anything to him. But the lad knows the islands are in the ocean — that's cool!

"You have to go to school."

"Just remember I was at a Kyiv high school! Dad, be honest! I speak Ukrainian day and night, even though we are not at Harvard. I have even taught your Dounia to say *hello* in Ukrainian!"

"So I've noticed. Well done!"

"Well, take me to the islands then!"

"The places you've been to at your age. At your age I…"

"That was in the days of the Sodding Union! Life is quite different nowadays. People from our high school have been abroad much more. I am not the most-travelled by any means. I'm not even amongst the first ten! Dad, take me to the Azores. I've got enough pocket money for a pizza. You won't be paying for me in the restaurants."

"You will be served in the restaurant just as I will; that isn't a problem. But you'll have to buy a business-class ticket."

"Dad, I grew up without a father to look after me; you abandoned me when I was a toddler! So now at least take me with you to the islands!" says Myroslav, playing his final trump card, and Eugene sits down at his computer and reaches the appropriate airline site. He confirms that a ticket is available for his son on the same flight, and he writes to the *Different Worlds: Contact Points Congress* to get them to book a twin room. They instantly reply that they have booked accommodation for him and his son in a suite with two televisions.

"Look at that! How are you supposed to watch two televisions at once?" commented Myroslav on the response from the organisers.

They landed at Santa Maria airport and were driven to the Terceira Hotel. Everything had been arranged so they could rest until the next day, considering the time lag. Eugene lies down in the bedroom.

"You settle down in the lounge," he tells his son, pouring himself a sleeping draught.

"No problema," replied Myroslav, switching on the television. "A pity I don't know any Portuguese. Actually, here's an English channel."

When Eugene went to the window in the morning, even he, accustomed as he was to impressive landscapes, felt his heart miss a beat: "Oh God, how beautiful!" They might well be in for that intellectual swagger, humanitarian froth, cross-linguistic wordplay, not always witty, and the boasting about places one had been, which is the life-blood of the programmatic leitmotiv at gatherings of this ilk, but for the sake of several minutes like this by a window overlooking the bay it was worth enjoying the earthly status which permitted you to come here. As a matter of fact, even at such futile spectacles of intellectual pretentiousness, bright ideas sometimes make themselves heard, transfixing those who are capable only of listening to themselves.

The first person he met was his fellow-countryman Dmytro Udalchuk, who he probably sees at gatherings like this most often. Once, in the early days after independence, it was Udalchuk who arranged his first visit to America for him.

"So you're interpreting? You could be a presenter at these meetings," says Udalchuk.

"Everybody has their own destiny and their own broad pathway," replies Eugene.

"You have to be able to alter your destiny, and to narrow down the pathway or broaden it, according to circumstances."

"We'll see, Mr Udalchuk, how you will broaden your pathway or narrow it down when you are sixty and they stop inviting you to these conferences. You don't appear to have achieved the status of an Uiko Kazhych."

"Perhaps it can be achieved if you leave this country," replied Udalchuk, pointing out the name *Ukraine* on his conference badge and changing the subject:

"Allow me to introduce you, Eugene; this is our colleague from Japan, Yukusai," — the Japanese bows politely — "He is in…"

"Do you think I am the last ignoramus not to know who Yukusai is?" says Eugene, as one almost always does in such situations.

Yukusai's face glowed with pleasure, despite his Samurai composure. Eugene does not know who Yukusai is, but he is very aware of the impact of this guileless expression.

Now here is Uiko Kazhych himself, the author of sociophile bestsellers, which he writes in simple English so as not to present translators with unnecessary difficulties. This is someone of such a calibre that everybody here present will afterwards mention the fact that Kazhych was at that conference. Or, more tellingly: "I participate in conferences attended by Kazhych!"

And here is Burukova — where would they be without her? The leading anti-communist of Eastern Europe, who at all gatherings of this sort not only seeks opportunities to dazzle with her rabid, dated anti-communist rhetoric, but also is overtly on the lookout for a one-night stand.

"Hello, Samarey," calls out Burukova. "Isn't your wife with you?"

Burukova was at their university, teaching one of the Anticommunist Studies courses.

"I've brought my son with me," replies Eugene. "Kazhych came on his own. Have you made his acquaintance yet?"

"You surprise me," replies Burukova. "Are you still unaware of Kazhych's proclivities? The likes of your son should be kept away from him; where is he, actually?"

Eugene does not want to introduce Myroslav to Burukova.

"My son has a proficiency in aikido. As for Kazhych, he's an old bumpkin, to be honest. But I didn't know he was gay. But here's Yukusai; also on his own, apparently."

"Oh, which one is Yukusai?" asks Burukova, changing her tone of voice and flicking a strand of hair off her forehead.

"Burukova, this isn't like you! Such an intellectual and you don't know of Yukusai?"

"Of course I've heard of him! I've read his work! I just meant I don't know him personally!"

At the plenary session there is one Russian who needs simultaneous interpreting, and a Bulgarian who has submitted his text in Russian. Eugene enters the interpreters' cabin, puts on his headset and draws the microphone towards his mouth. He is already equipped to translate all those *challenges of the day*, *cultural hierarchies*, *kitschy structures*, *cases of the subconscious mind* and much else besides. He is also equipped to handle incomplete phrases and he has learnt to pick up a thought expressed in poor English, something not everybody has the ability to do. He was gratified when he succeeded in this and he did not mind when the audience at the congress began applauding the speaker and not him. A grateful glance from the speaker was enough for him. When someone starts speaking Russian in fits and starts, he translates these fragmented phrases so that the audience can hear the idea emerging out of the swirling ungainliness. He enjoys this work, although he knows that Udalchuk is right: to boast "I saw Kazhych" is the same as if some sound technician were to boast that he set up the microphones for the Scorpions, say.

It's a pity he did not study German to the same level. It's a pity there are few opportunities to interpret from Ukrainian. People from Ukraine either speak Russian or they endeavour to speak English, with differing degrees of success. Incidentally, who else is there from Ukraine this time, apart from Udalchuk?

He examines the programme. Here is a list of the presentations at the plenary. The last one is by a woman from Ukraine. *Tatiana Maroukhina. The nerve of existence of small nations.* Hell's bells, there's a topic for you! What's her name? There's never been anything like that before. He reads more carefully… These Slavonic surnames transliterated into the Roman alphabet aren't always transparent, not even to his experienced eye. *Tatiana Ma-rou…* Right, now he has to read the presentation by the Bulgarian who gave him the text in Russian but who will speak from the rostrum in Bulgarian… That item is finished now. Now other interpreters will take over, and he will read more closely who this speaker from Ukraine is…

… If all this is being filmed for some cosmic archives of events, let the sound track play Vivaldi's *Storm*! *Tatiana Maroukhina*! I believe Mykhailo Tykhonovych from Pskov gave this surname to his daughters Tanya and Olya; he wanted to call them Marusya and Oksana, but his wife Zoya Mykolayivna, the stubborn Ukie, insisted on naming them in honour of Pushkin. It may not be her; there are countless people with this same name all over the world. But if there once was an inherited house and two sisters who were so unalike, and the fiancé of one of them, and the birthday celebrations, and a 'duel', then there also ought to be a gathering of the nobility where a naïve, brainless, rural girl turns up in a different guise, transubstantiated, representing one more hypostasis of the eternal recurrence, Ewige Wiederkunft, which he had read about at that time, in the house he inherited; he had read on until he reached a state of self-oblivion, physically sensing the vortices of the time strata at the site of the ancient site of the sorcerers' sabbath.

Eugene removes his headphones, leaves the glass cabin, makes for the conference hall and surveys the people present. The presenters usually sit in the front row. Here she is. She has changed, but he recognises her. An elegant jacket, an attractive hairstyle and an earnest demeanour. That is exactly how they look when they still think great ideas are born at gatherings like this. She must be thirty by now. She looks very young. A very likeable lady. At this point, the genre requires him to fall at her feet. But he feels light-hearted. Postmodern is postmodern. Reading great themes today does not evoke exhilaration, but it does evoke laughter. So the story of his life has to be such a monumental piece of Russian kitsch!

On the rostrum, the next intellectual speaks in German; quite an astute man, Eugene knows him. Some participants are listening to him without headphones, but most are wearing them, listening to the English or the Russian translation. Tanya, in the front row, has not put on her headphones. Does she know German? On the other hand, as she is about to give her own presentation she may not be listening to the others; he notices that she is gripping the print-out of her talk nervously.

He walks quietly along the corridor beneath the glass partition beyond which the sea is roaring, displaying the grand drama of the raging Atlantic. The seats are not all occupied; he is offered a place and he quietly indicates he doesn't need one. But he asks for another copy of the programme, because he has left his in the cabin.

There were two final presentations remaining. Tatiana Maroukhina had not specified that she required an interpreter. But she might get stuck with her English; he had met this many times. Perhaps he should offer to help? So while the audience is applauding the German, he sits down next to Tanya in the front row and asks her, just managing to restrain a smile:

"Will you be speaking in English, madam? Will you be requiring any assistance?"

After he had spoken he regretted it, because his presence disturbed her. She is already nervous, and now an old acquaintance makes an inopportune re-appearance.

"You're balding," she says, finally.

"You're quite right. But the moustache is still there."

He no longer offers his services, sitting in silence next to her in the front row. Now it's the penultimate presentation, and Burukova starts bellowing on about how the Soviet occupation forces repressed her sexuality. Then it's the turn of Tatiana Maroukhina. Isn't she married? Has she kept the surname of her dad from Pskov?

Tanya went up to the rostrum; he sat on the stage by the microphone, occupying the end chair next to the rostrum, where an interpreter sits who is there merely to assist the speaker. Tanya's voice is shaky. But she speaks quite well. Would he have paid such close attention to her presentation if it was not for the personal connection? Perhaps not. But, bearing in mind the context, this sounds simply brilliant!

"Small nations may occupy quite an extensive territory, but nevertheless they are small, because they generate neither great ideas nor great people. More exactly, people achieve greatness when they go to great countries. Best of all — to America. They go in quest of self-fulfilment, but quite often, on their way across the Atlantic, they lose that vital flame which drove them abroad in search of their identity.

But America itself has also given the world so many dissatisfied, impassioned personalities, such as Ernest Hemingway, who so many years after his death still obliges people to talk about him. Small nations also have figures like Hemingway. But the world is unfamiliar with them. This is not because there are no translators or literary agents to make Eastern European Hemingways visible to the world. Rather it is because the American Hemingway is enough for the entire world. However, this does not mean that Eastern Europeans who have sensed within themselves that impulse, that will to live and that intense affinity with their own culture, should either re-construct themselves and undertake some great imperial, big-nation project, or suppress this flame, lamenting the unfavourable political situation. It is not to do with emigration. Even in emigration you can fulfil your task within the framework of your native culture, and even in your native country you can fail to achieve anything.

To lament the ignorance, the lack of understanding in small nations, their insignificance, from the rostrum of a gathering such as this, has long since become commonplace. But the blank wall of insignificance can only be penetrated if one rejects the commonplace, the vocabulary of sweeping generalisations, sweeping ideas, if one becomes an independent personality, rather than declaring one's adaptability to the spirit of History. This is precisely what Milan Kundera, perhaps the most brilliant intellectual of Eastern Europe, an émigré, as a matter of fact, wrote about in his novel *Immortality*.

"It isn't from *Immortality*, it's from *Testaments Betrayed*," said Eugene, correcting her with a smile. In America he had once failed to find a copy of *Immortality* in Russian, which he had not finished reading, so he had bought it in English. The same went for other books by this extraordinary Czech.

Tanya thanked him for the correction; yes, of course, it is from *Testaments Betrayed*, not from *Immortality*. Initially, Tanya was put off her stride, but then she forgot that the audience, including quite well-known people, judged emotional young women severely. She even forgot that he was next to her, although the presentation was addressed to him, the man she had once declared her love for, whose books, forgotten in his fear, she had gradually been reading very attentively, so as one day to be his equal.

"Goethe said: *Werde der du bist*, — become who you are. Later, this thought was taken up with a vengeance by Nietzsche. This coincides with the fact that it is the core of any religion: to comprehend one's vocation, which is not easy, and then to fulfil that vocation, which is incredibly demanding. Indeed, it is possible to achieve this only on condition that you will not be afraid of there being no recompense during your lifetime and of its being forgotten when you are dead!"

"Bravo, Tanya! Who would have thought it? This is better than marrying a general, the hero of 1812! ... Incidentally, how are things at the General's house?"

Tanya was enthusiastically applauded. Perhaps it was cynical applause greeting the end of the plenary session, after which everybody was in for a sumptuous lunch. It could be that the impassioned voice of the young speaker had created a few ripples at this largely predictable meeting. They congratulated her, pressed their business cards into her hand, and an informal discussion of her paper was proposed, to follow the evening session. In the bar or somewhere.

The interpreters were served separately, so he did not see Tanya at the lunch. Afterwards, he was interpreting for one section while Tanya was participating in a different one. Then he had dinner with the organisers in a small circle at which Tanya was not present. Naturally, he was interpreting more than eating or drinking. On the following day he was interpreting at a round table discussion for the first half of the day, and the second half was devoted to a big reception given by the governor of the island of Terceira, where he had met up with Tanya at last. They did not have much time to chat. People were offering compliments to Tanya and to Eugene, telling him he was the best interpreter. Burukova quipped that she would immediately telephone Dounia and tell her about his charming friend. Yukusai asked Eugene where he had heard his name mentioned. He replied that Yukusai's name was so significant in the present context that the original source was lost in the mists of time. But he and Tanya nevertheless did have a chance to be alone together over drinks, sitting on a large window-sill in the corridor.

"I am very happy for you, my dear."

"And I am infinitely grateful to you."

"For what, Tanya?"

"Firstly, that you did not defile me fifteen years ago."

"And all those years I thought the sexual rejection had been traumatic for you."

"Secondly, I am grateful that you were so scared after you had beaten up Volodya that you ran away, leaving your books behind. Kundera, Nietzsche and the German textbooks. And the bilingual text of *Eugene Onegin* too."

"Tanya, hang on! You said I *beat him up*!!!"

"How else can I put it? He was in a coma for several days;

then he revived, but he couldn't recognise anybody. After that he continued to get better and now he is fully recovered, long since."

"I have lived all these years with the burden of having involuntarily killed someone!"

"I drove back from the station burdened with a similar thought. I told myself I had saved you, but I had left him on the frozen ground by the barn, just at the place where my dad had built the concrete steps. But Olya had gone to his side."

"Olya at Volodya's side?"

"When we all went outside — well, you remember all that..."

"I remember, Tanya; how could I forget?"

"It was on the same day as our birthday that a telegram arrived and was read out aloud, saying that you were expected at the American embassy. Nobody thought I was rescuing Volodya's murderer, no — I was driving you to the station so you would make it to the US embassy the next day. Olya realised that you were going to America, so she immediately switched back to Volodya. Olya looked after him the whole time, giving up her studies. Later, she rejoined the second year and graduated from the college of medicine a year later."

"How are things otherwise in 'our' village?" asked Eugene with a smile.

"Olya and Volodya are married."

"Have they got any children?"

"Three. They live in your house. Although Volodya has had a place built now. But they haven't moved in yet. Volodya said it was in your house, on the site of the sorcerers' sabbath, that he recovered completely from his head injury."

"The ancient Kobi knew where to brew their potion..."

"Actually, that house belongs to you. What about coming over to sort out your property!"

"Oh, let them carry on living there!"

"No! Volodya can't help feeling he is living in somebody else's house. They will move out soon, and the house will stand empty once more and become a ruin, as it was before your General moved in, which is a shame. As a matter of fact, nobody has ever lived in the north wing, and the children were not allowed to go in there. It has always been a museum."

"A museum?"

"The General's and yours. Volodya transferred all the notes the General made into there. There was no question of throwing them all on the fire."

"Actually, I wanted to read them one day…"

"If you're up for it, they're waiting… Volodya moved the General's bookcase and that sideboard to the sitting room in the north wing as well, so as not to damage his magnificent monogram dinner service which awaits your grand arrival in person."

"Oh my goodness!"

"That's right! All those things that you left behind at the time are still there. Including the photograph of some attractive woman on the desk."

"That's the General's first wife."

"Really? For a long time I wondered whose photograph that was … Everything is there, just as you left it: the books, the CD player and the typewriter on the window-sill…"

"So it really is a museum…"

"And your leather jacket on the back of the chair. And your five million coupons in the soup tureen."

"But why didn't you spend them on something you wanted? They were legal tender then!"

"Straight afterwards, I couldn't! I couldn't even bring myself to touch them. By the time I could, they were worthless, and there was no way I could exchange them."

Footsteps were heard in the corridor.

"Mr Samarsky, there you are! At last! The mayor is looking for you. That man from Russia has arrived; your assistance is essential!"

That's right, he is at work now, so he is not allowed to weaken, unlike the conference delegates. Eugene hurries to the hall, because the Russian billionaire who generously financed this sumptuous celebration of the intellect has arrived and he wants to speak with the organisers. Apparently, his own interpreters cannot cope. Eugene takes his leave of Tanya, handing her his business card, but his son Myroslav hurries towards her with the greeting *Guten Tag, Tatiana Mikaelivna!*

"How do you know her?" Eugene asks his son on the plane during their return flight.

"She taught German at our high school. And she ran the German philosophy option."

"Well, it turns out Kyiv is still a big village, where at any party, even outside Kyiv, the denizens meet, if not their friends, at any rate the friends of their friends."

"How do you know her?" asks Myroslav.

"Oh, I've only just met her."

"So why did she ask after you when she was our teacher? She asked me if I was your son. I said I was. Well, aren't I?"

"But why did she ask you about that, of all things, out of the blue?"

"Man! You gave me your surname! Have you forgotten?"

The food and wine is served. Myroslav orders wine:

"Red wine, please!"

"You are too young to drink wine," says Eugene, pretending to adopt the tone of an overbearing father; for himself, he orders a whisky.

"I don't drive yet."

"But Tanya did, at your age." Eugene does not say this out loud — he keeps this to himself, as he contemplates what an attractive woman Tanya has become. He could go for her, of course he could. But could he have any expectations? Actually, he was quite perturbed about how earlier events had turned out, in the end. Indeed, as time went by he found it increasingly disturbing. It would be an exaggeration to speak of his being battered by *a storm of emotions*, but for the moment he is even unable to eat. Of course, the most enjoyable thing about plane journeys is the food, and he always relishes the fact that life does not oblige him to fly with budget airlines, which do not serve meals. He tries to calm down, taking out his smartphone; after all, this is no time to be taking a sleeping pill. He is in business class, so he has internet access. While Myroslav is chomping on his lunch, Eugene checks his mail.

Dear Zhenia!

In the relations between us everything has always been as in the timeless Russian novel, except for Tatiana's letter to Eugene. So I am correcting that omission. My flight is eastbound in the evening and you are already on your way westwards. We did not finish that conversation in the corridor at the governor's offices, so here are a few lines for you, to catch up. I am grateful to you for not exploiting a little girl's stupidity. I am grateful that you left your books behind in the General's house. Next to them lies to this day the issue of the 'Gardener's News', now turned yellow, that contained the rudimentary little article on Nietzsche, against which you wrote a comment in Russian: "What a stupid girl!" I cried so much over that! I don't know what the fortune-teller Demyanivna told you. She told me you were the one who marked out my fate, and every day after school I came to your house and tried to read your books. I couldn't manage them, but I kept on reading anyway, so that one day I would meet you, but not as a 'stupid girl'. I put Nietzsche aside and began turning the pages of Milan Kundera's 'Immortality'. I was surprised to find there exactly what you had bombarded my parents with about the Russians' 'pre-coital love'. Almost word for word. So these were not your ideas. But it meant that if I read books I might become interesting to you later on.

But how was it possible to get through the dreadful black two-volume work containing a portrait of a man with a large moustache and burning eyes? I could tell from the way the pages were worn that you spent the most time reading 'Ecce homo'. This two-volume set still lies on your desk. And to this day I read those texts in different editions, although, as you know, Nietzsche can never be read right through to the end.

And I am grateful too for those words you called out to me as you clambered aboard the train, when we both thought Volodya had perished. You shouted out that after a while Olya wouldn't be able to get through the doorway. It isn't quite like that, but she is now about twice the size she was. She is attractive, though, none the less, and Volodya loves her.

But what about the butterfly on her behind? Is it twice the size too? Has she who *would become a good mother to the children and a faithful wife to her husband* had it removed? Eugene looked up from the letter and noticed his son had finished his meal, and that he had enjoyed it.

"Have mine as well," he said to Myroslav, returning to the letter.

You called out to me that I would be attractive and sensible and that we would meet up in the middle of the Atlantic. Perhaps you have forgotten what you told me then. But you were sincere in wanting to say something kind to the young girl who was rescuing you, and you said it with such passion that everything has come true, especially the Atlantic. You did not predict the future; you brought it about by the power of your words. Thank you from the bottom of my heart!

But where is the "end I am afraid to re-read"? It happens that a text is written for the sake of its last line, blazing on the horizon in fiery letters. But once the text of life is written, that line turns out to be superfluous…

30th April — 17th June 2012

Glagoslav Publications Catalogue

- *The Time of Women* by Elena Chizhova
- *Sin* by Zakhar Prilepin
- *Hardly Ever Otherwise* by Maria Matios
- *The Lost Button* by Irene Rozdobudko
- *Khatyn* by Ales Adamovich
- *Christened with Crosses* by Eduard Kochergin
- *The Vital Needs of the Dead* by Igor Sakhnovsky
- *METRO 2033* (Dutch Edition) by Dmitry Glukhovsky
- *METRO 2034* (Dutch Edition) by Dmitry Glukhovsky
- *A Poet and Bin Laden* by Hamid Ismailov
- *Asystole* by Oleg Pavlov
- *Kobzar* by Taras Shevchenko
- *White Shanghai* by Elvira Baryakina
- *The Stone Bridge* by Alexander Terekhov
- *King Stakh's Wild Hunt* by Uladzimir Karatkevich
- *Depeche Mode* by Serhii Zhadan
- *Saraband Sarah's Band* by Larysa Denysenko
- *Herstories*, An Anthology of New Ukrainian Women Prose Writers
- *Watching The Russians* (Dutch Edition) by Maria Konyukova
- *The Hawks of Peace* by Dmitry Rogozin
- *The Grand Slam and Other Stories* (Dutch Edition) by Leonid Andreev
- *The Battle of the Sexes Russian Style* by Nadezhda Ptushkina
- *A Book Without Photographs* by Sergei Shargunov

More coming soon…